The Guy, the Girl, the Artist and His Ex

The Guy, the Girl, the Artist and His Ex

GABRIELLE WILLIAMS

Groundwood Books
House of Anansi Press
Toronto Berkeley

Groundwood Books / House of Anansi Press
groundwoodbooks.com

We acknowledge for their financial support of our publishing program the Government of Canada.

With the participation of the Government of Canada
Avec la participation du gouvernement du Canada | Canadä

Library and Archives Canada Cataloguing in Publication
Williams, Gabrielle, author
The guy, the girl, the artist and his ex / Gabrielle Williams.
First published in Australia in 2015 by Allen & Unwin.
Issued in print and electronic formats.
ISBN 978-1-55498-941-6 (paperback) .— ISBN 978-1-55498-942-3
(epub).—ISBN 978-1-55498-943-0 (mobi)
I. Title.
PR9619.4.W54G89 2017   j823'.92   C2016-905751-8
C2016-905752-6

Cover design and interior design by Michael Solomon
Cover illustration by Alessandra Olanow

Groundwood Books is committed to protecting our natural environment. As part of our efforts, the interior of this book is printed on paper that contains 100% post-consumer recycled fibers, is acid-free and is processed chlorine-free.

Printed and bound in Canada

For my guy,
from your girl.

On August 2, 1986, a group calling itself the Australian Cultural Terrorists stole one of the world's most iconic paintings — Picasso's *Weeping Woman* — off the walls of the National Gallery of Victoria and held it for ransom, demanding an increase in government funding for artists in Victoria. The painting was the subject of an international manhunt involving Interpol, Scotland Yard and the Australian Federal Police.

The Australian Cultural Terrorists were never found.

LETTERS TO THE EDITOR

Friday, August 15, 1986

Thank heavens

Thank heavens that monstrosity has been taken off the walls of our gallery.

Eileen Porter, Balwyn

Problem solved

Stolen Picasso? No problem — we can easily get another one by holding a competition among Victoria's kindergarten children. Who knows, we might end up with the entire Picasso collection.

Bob Frampton, Bacchus Marsh

About time

It's about time someone stood up for the thousands of grossly underfunded artists in this state. A ten percent increase in funding would hardly blow the budget and is virtually what was demanded in the Botsman Report.

Rosemary Lake, Clifton Hill

Before the party but
after the theft

The Guy

G uy Lethlean considered it to be one of life's great piss-offs: the fact a person could be genuinely good at a thing that had absolutely no use in the world whatsoever.

A thing that wouldn't get you good marks at school.

That wouldn't get you into uni.

That you couldn't make any money out of.

And that you couldn't be world champion of.

The hacky sack, for example.

Guy could keep that little bean-filled sack off the ground — bouncing from foot to foot, up the shin, round the back, off his ankle, knee, chest — the longest out of anyone he knew. His record was seven minutes, forty-three seconds.

He was basically unbeatable.

If the hacky sack was a horse race, he'd be hands-down champion of the Melbourne Cup.

If the hacky sack was a swimming race, he'd have a bunch of Olympic gold medals around his neck.

Unfortunately, the hacky sack was a bag of beans, and that was about as much value as it had in the world.

Guy was on a Melbourne Cup-worthy streak of hacky sacking with Benj at the park down the road from his house. The sun was headed for the other side of the world behind the chilly chimney tops of the Melbourne horizon, and the August afternoon had turned wintry dark.

Benj punted the little ball off his ankle in Guy's direction, then leaned down and hoisted his schoolbag onto his shoulder. His long fringe obscured his face with the lean-down, then flicked back out of his eyes with the hoist-up.

"I gotta split," Benj said, looking up at the ominous clouds. "Need to do some study before I come back round to yours."

Guy pocketed the hacky sack like he hadn't even noticed how good he was at the world's most useless sport.

The two of them walked up the hill to their respective houses, as the streetlights cranked up and the rain started pissing down.

Unlike Benj, Guy didn't spend the rest of the afternoon studying.

Wasn't much point.

He was too far gone.

He wasn't going to blitz his exams. In fact, there was a fair chance he wasn't even going to pass them. So instead, he shucked off his school uniform, pulled on a T-shirt and some shorts and went for a run in the storm.

Down Rockley Road, through the hacky-sack park, right at Toorak Road, T-shirt soaked already, left into Chapel Street, past shops with names like Indigo and Saba and Sempre L'Unico.

At the end of last year, Guy had done a very bad thing.

Or, not so much bad as … stupid.

Or, not necessarily stupid. More … very clever. If it had worked out as planned. Which it hadn't.

It had gone all right initially, but now here he was, months down the track, stuck with the very bad/stupid/smart-if-it-had-worked-out thing he'd done and not sure where to go with it.

Over Malvern Road, past Pran Central, over High Street — the buildings changing in that single crossing from expensive boutiques to cheap rental housing and tired shopfronts that no one bothered with.

The cold rain felt aggressive in his face, but good on his sweating body.

Over Dandenong Road, past the Astor Theatre with its thirty-year-old movies and fifty-year-old foyer, down the hill, past the police station, the rooming houses, past the sad old guys not caring about the rain, only caring about the brown paper bags they were clutching to their chests.

It had been the Christmas holidays. Nine months ago.

End of Year Eleven.

Guy's school report had turned up.

He wouldn't normally have seen it until after his mum and dad had gone through it, but this was one of those postman-delivers-the-mail-as-you're-walking-through-the-front-gate type arrangements, and when Guy saw the school crest on the envelope there wasn't a question that he wouldn't open it. It was his report, after all. He had a right to know.

As he flicked through the pages, he wasn't able to help noticing: *Guy's lack of organization and commitment has prevented him from achieving at a satisfactory level,* for maths.

D.

And: *Guy has not attempted to engage with the course content or submit assignment work and has not been prepared to seek help or guidance,* for science.

D.

And, for English: *Guy has struggled to commit himself. He has not been able to concentrate on class discussions, becoming easily distracted. In order to improve, Guy needs to focus clearly on what is being discussed in class and ask questions if he is unsure of the task.*

D.

Not good.

The idea of binning the entire report occurred to him. He could pretend it had never come. The postman hadn't delivered it. The school forgot to send it.

But then another idea quickly rose to the surface of his brain, like some kind of glutinous swamp bubble. Thick and juicy and full of steam. A brilliant, stupendous idea that would sort things out for now and give him the breathing space he needed to fix his marks before his next report arrived in the letter box at the end of first term, Year Twelve.

He unstapled the pages of his report, whited out the incriminating marks and comments, went to the library, photocopied each whited out page so it looked fresh, re-typed less incriminating marks and comments onto the photocopied pages, stapled the pages carefully back into the official school folder, slid the new improved version back into the official school envelope and left it on the kitchen bench for his folks to retrieve when they got home.

Guy has committed himself to English this term — delete "struggled to" — *Guy focuses clearly on what is being discussed in class and asks questions if he is unsure of the task.*

B.

Very nice.

For maths: *Guy's organization* — delete the words "lack of" — *and commitment have seen him achieving at a satisfactory level.*

B.

For science: *Guy has engaged with the course content and submitted excellent* — he thought he'd throw in an "excellent" for good measure — *assignment work.*

B.

And so on and so forth for each subject of Year Eleven.

He toyed with the idea of giving himself a couple of As, but then his dad wouldn't have anything to complain about. Besides, the Bs were a good get-out-of-jail-free card but they weren't an oversell on the amount of homework the old man had seen him doing over the past few months.

The other good thing about the Bs was that he felt certain he'd be able to achieve them by the time his next report came in the mail. Every forged B he'd given himself had simply been a commitment to the genuine Bs he was going to get the following term, and that couldn't be a bad thing.

In fact, looked at from certain viewpoints (okay, one viewpoint — his), forging his school report had been a noble act. It had been Guy's commitment to a better version of himself.

Left onto Nepean Highway, the homeward-bound traffic bonnet-to-boot, bonnet-to-boot, headlights on, windscreen wipers cutting a swath through the rain only to have more rain dump down — a pointless but necessary exercise.

Guy was hitting the rhythmic, orchestral part of his run, when each touch-down of his foot was the briefest pawing at the ground. The rest of the time, his forward momentum defied the rules of gravity. His arms were pistons and his chest was pumping in and out like bellows, and these were the moments he ran for, when every element of his body worked exactly as it was designed to work.

Hunting moments, was how he thought of them. Moments when he could have caught a wild animal if he was a native in the jungle.

Then the traffic lights at Nepean Highway blocked him. The beauty of the run — the drugged, euphoric moment of it — stopped, and he was back with two feet concreted to the earth.

Year Twelve hadn't panned out the way Guy had hoped. He'd found it hard to concentrate at school. He would zone out in the middle (okay, right at the beginning) of each class, and only zone back in when the school bell rang for recess, or lunch, or home time. He couldn't sit still at his desk when he got home each day. Study was impossible. Assignments were worse. He wasn't able to get anywhere near those genuine Bs he'd been aiming for.

In good news, though, his hacky-sack skills had come along a treat.

At the end of first term, Year Twelve, Guy hijacked the postman at the front gate, went to the library, photocopied the pages of his report, made a few adjustments, and was good to go.

Straight Bs again.

Guy couldn't lay claim to any noble motivation for that report. It was a simple matter of frantic arse-covering.

He turned right into New Street, then left past the park, where a candidate for Dog Owner of the Year stood in the squalling weather calling out to a dog that seemed to be completely ignoring him.

Guy would have loved a dog of his own to take running with him. In fact, he and his mum both would have loved one, but his dad was a no-go zone on the whole dog-ownership issue. When his dad looked at a dog, instead of seeing a potential pet for the family, all he saw was fur (all over the couch), saliva (dragged across his pant leg) and poo (in the backyard). He didn't see the sweet, soulful eyes, or the smiling mouth, or the perky ears. Nope. Fur, saliva, poo. The sum total, according to his dad, of most dogs.

The dog was now running in the opposite direction from Dog Owner of the Year. Deliberately, it would seem. Perhaps even gleefully.

Guy grinned. You had to love dogs.

He turned right at Head Street, running down to the beach, then along the empty, sodden beach footpath.

The big guns were aimed directly at his head now, with the pressure of getting-into-university-type exams approaching, and he was going to have to tell his parents sometime soon that he wasn't going as well as they thought he was.

That there wasn't a hope in hell he'd get the marks he needed for any of the courses his folks wanted him to do (those courses consisting of law at Melbourne Uni like his dad, or law at Melbourne Uni like his dad).

Left at Bay Street, up past the Dev Hotel. Past more houses, then along the shopping strip, the rain relentless, drenched people hauling bags of supermarket shopping out of their trolleys and into the boots of their cars. Left at Nepean Highway. Back toward the city.

He knew he had to tell his folks what he'd done, but every time an opportunity presented itself, he backed down.

Take this weekend, for example. His parents had gone skiing with some friends. Left Guy home alone so he could get "stuck into the books" now that the "business end of the year," as his old man called it, was approaching. He could have told them before they left earlier this afternoon.

You know what? he could have said. *I might as well come skiing with you guys because, to be honest, school's not going that great.*

They would have protested. They would have pointed to his reports as proof that he was coming along okay.

Sure, his dad would have said, *Bs aren't exactly what we're after, but just keep studying, mate* — and here he would have clapped Guy on the shoulder, all friendly, as if there wasn't a problem, no pressure, just do your best, get straight As — *and you'll be fine.*

He wasn't going to be fine.

Although he still clung to the hope that somehow he would get away with it. That something fluke-ish would come along and fix things for him. That he would never have to tell, and they would never have to find out.

Who knew? Maybe when it came to the actual exams he'd get all these amazing marks. He'd cram a year's worth of study into the two weeks of swot vac, and on the days of the exams, it'd be straight As. Or straight Bs, at least. His teachers wouldn't be able to believe how well he'd done. He'd even have trouble believing it himself, but the marks would be there, on the letter from the Education Department, telling him that he was a legend.

And those forged Bs? Well, no one needed to know.

Or maybe the school would burn down, and all the records would be lost, and the exams would be postponed for a year, and by that stage he'd be studying like a brainiac and As would be yawningly easy. And law at Melbourne Uni? They'd be begging him to attend.

Or maybe he would die before exams started. Some kind of freak accident. Something sad and tragic that would leave his folks bereft and crying and none the wiser about his little forgery. Also, nothing too painful, because he didn't want it to hurt as he carked it.

He kept going along the highway, ignoring the Chapel Street turnoff, opting instead to go through St. Kilda Junction and then along leafy, expansive St. Kilda Road for the home stretch.

The thing was, if he had told his parents the truth before they went skiing, they sure as shit wouldn't have left him home alone for the weekend to study. His dad would have stayed in Melbourne, sporting his angry face. His mum would have hung around the house, her disappointed face there whenever she served a meal or put a dish in the dishwasher. And the fact was, Guy didn't want to have to deal with either face just yet.

Plus, he wanted the house all to himself.

Without his folks around, it didn't matter if the dishes weren't washed, if there were clothes and crap in the lounge room, if he went for a run for a couple of hours, if he didn't get up till lunchtime.

If he didn't even bother pretending to study.

He turned right into Toorak Road, past Fawkner Park where his dad played tennis every Thursday night with his lawyer pals. Past Christchurch Grammar, where Guy had gone to school as a little kid.

21

He might be a forger and failing school and only good at hacky sack, but Guy Lethlean wasn't insane. And that's what he would have had to be, to tell his folks the score before they went skiing.

Give up this weekend?

No parents in the house?

He wasn't telling them nothin' — at least until after they got back.

The Girl

R afi knew all about drowning.

There'd been that little girl who used to hang around out in front of the school in La Paz, waiting for her older sister to finish her lessons so they could walk home together. Found facedown in an irrigation ditch one afternoon, barely any water in it. Drowned.

There'd been the ten-month-old baby in the apartment block next door to Rafi's place in Calle Omasuyos, who'd sunk to the bottom of the bath while his mother's back was turned. Twenty seconds — apparently that was all it took.

There was Renata Romero — a couple of years above Rafi at school — who'd gone out with friends one weekend. Her body had been found days later in the Chametla-El Centenario saltmarsh.

And then, of course, there was Tonio. Rafi's three-year-old brother.

All of them drowned. By La Llorona, the horse-headed woman of South American legend.

Ten years later, thousands of kilometers away from Chametla-El Centenario and La Paz and Tonio, Rafi sat at the kitchen table in Melbourne, Australia, the rain beating a steady tattoo on the roof.

Her pens were neatly arranged in front of her, her folder open to a fresh page, her pristine maths book propped open at page twenty-seven. Formulae she'd written down for easy reference were at her elbow, and picture after picture of La Llorona surrounded her.

She hadn't drawn any of them — she was strictly a maths-and-science girl herself. But over the past few months, her mum had become obsessed with drawing and painting and sketching and sculpting, over and over, the horse-headed figure of La Llorona, and the images had taken over the flat: Wanted posters for Rafi's brother's murderer.

There were horse-headed figures drawn on flattened-out cardboard boxes, streaky crayons on newspaper, drizzled watercolors on lined exercise books, sculptures made out of plasticine and air-drying clay. There was a life-sized horse's head made out of papier-mâché that you could put over your shoulders and actually wear (if you ever happened to be in the mood, which Rafi doubted she ever would be). There were even tiny white models made out of Minties: a whole collection of miniature (Minty-ature) horse-headed women set up on the windowsill of the lounge room.

But then, a couple of weeks ago, her mum had stopped — put down her paints and brushes and not picked them up again.

Just like that. Simple as turning off a tap.

This had happened before. This compulsive painting thing. After Tonio died all those years back, after the funeral, when Rafi, her mum and her stepdad, Ferdi, were trying to settle into the new routine of being a family of three instead of a family of four, Rafi's mum overran their house with drawings and paintings and sketches and carvings of La Llorona, a watery hoofprint drip-drip-dripping through every room.

Rafi would come home from school to find Ferdi — Tonio's devastated dad — stuffing bundles of still-wet paintings into the bin. He would tell Rafi that her mum was so *terrible-mente, terriblemente triste* — terribly, terribly sad — about Tonio that she was painting La Llorona over and over until she got it straight in her head.

Rafi's mum would sit in the same spot at their kitchen table every day until — as if the darkness inside her head was spilling out through her ears and over her shoulders and into their little house — the night would take over the room.

And still she'd draw the same image over and over again.

But the pictures hadn't straightened her head out.

Instead, she'd gone further and further inside her skull, until she reached a place where it was just the three of them: her, Tonio and La Llorona.

At that point, Rafi's stepdad stopped coming home.

Rafi would come home from school, from primary school, and make bread-and-garlic soup for dinner, or hominy stew, or corn-masa cakes — well, her version of these dishes: a simpler, more basic, cooked-by-a-seven-year-old version. Food that was only eaten by the seven-year-old in the house, her mother refusing everything. Eating nothing.

After she made dinner, Rafi would go outside and play with her friends. Then she'd come inside a little later on and draw her own versions of La Llorona — the horse-headed woman taking Tonio and stealing him away, spying on Rafi

25

from the other side of the river, waiting for the right time to take her as well.

One day, Rafi's uncle Real came to visit, all the way from Melbourne in Australia. Rafi didn't know him very well at that stage, seeing as he lived on the other side of the world from her.

He was tall and very carefully dressed, wearing a buttoned-up suit with the tiniest triangle of a handkerchief poking out of the top pocket. His hair was slicked back, the ridges created by his comb still visible.

He was on his way to an art fair in Colombia, he said, and had decided to drop in to La Paz to see how they were going. To see how they were managing.

To see if they were okay.

He picked his way through the paintings and drawings that were flooding their house, now that Ferdi wasn't there to stem the flow. He saw the piled-up saucepans in the sink that Rafi barely washed before cooking with them again. The gloomy, curtained rooms.

Uncle Real pulled out some airplane tickets he'd brought with him — tickets for her and her mum.

He told Rafi that in Melbourne she would be close to him and her uncle Moritz. She would love it there, he said. They had kangaroos and koalas, he told her. She would have *una vida feliz* — a happy life — living in the flat upstairs from Uncle Moritz's bistro.

He said that when they left La Paz her mum would stop drawing La Llorona. That he and Uncle Moritz would help her stop.

He'd lied about the kangaroos and koalas. There were none. Not walking down the street, and not living in the trees.

But the rest of it? The happy life? The drawings stopping? He'd been absolutely spot on.

That day back in La Paz.

There hadn't been a hint, a flicker, a single solitary heads-up that something bad was about to happen. In fact, if anything it had been a great day, fun, one of the best ever, right up until that very last moment.

They'd gone to La Feria del Caballo — the Horse Fair.

People were dressed up. Chili butter from the corn-on-a-stick dripped down Rafi's chin. Her stepdad's hand engulfed her own.

Spangled women rode feet first on barebacked horses, their arms outstretched like it was no big deal, like they always rode horses this way.

Rodeo riders flipped and flopped like rag dolls on furious, arching, stamping stallions.

Everybody was happy. Everyone was having a good time. And then like a rip down a bolt of fabric, Rafi's mum came wailing through the crowd, a dripping wet, blue-lipped Tonio in her arms.

Later on, Rafi's mum would say she'd seen a woman with a horse's head that afternoon, half an hour before Tonio drowned, but when she looked a second time, she thought it was a trick of her eyes. A woman was bent next to a fence, a horse leaned over the fence, and the two of them merged for that brief moment.

"But then later when I looked around for Tonio and saw people running toward the stables," she would say, her voice watery, "I knew straight away that La Llorona had taken him.

It wasn't a trick of my eyes. It was her, wandering around the fair, looking for a child to take."

And Rafi's brother had been her number-one pick.

"Hay muchas versiones diferentes," Rafi's uncle Morrie used to say when Rafi first moved to Melbourne. "There are many different versions."

Every time he came to their flat, Rafi would ask him to tell her the story.

"La Llorona was very beautiful," he would begin, tucking Rafi's hair behind her ear. "She was poor, but she had the face of an angel. As a young woman not even out of her teens, La Llorona fell in love with a young man in her village and they had two little children together. They were poor but happy. But then he died, and La Llorona had to go and work in one of the big houses just out of town. The house was owned by one of the wealthiest men in the district, and his son couldn't keep his eyes off La Llorona, nor could she keep hers off him. They would steal moments away from the house together, and La Llorona thought it was love.

"One day, the son told her he was getting married — that his father had arranged a marriage to the daughter of a wealthy family from the next village. La Llorona was devastated. Her lover explained to her that he would never have been able to marry her because, apart from anything else, she had had two children with another man. He told La Llorona that he had to do the right thing by his family.

"La Llorona was desperately in love," Uncle Morrie would tell Rafi as she cuddled up on his lap. "She became obsessed with the idea that her two children were holding her back.

So she took her babies down to the river one afternoon and threw them into the water, even though they were too small to swim. Then she went back to her lover and told him what she'd done — that she didn't have her children anymore, she'd gotten rid of them, and he could marry her now that she was free. No responsibilities. No children.

"He, of course," Uncle Morrie would continue, the Spanish words purring deep inside his chest against Rafi's ear, "was horrified by what La Llorona had done. He ran to the river and tried to save the children, but he was too late. La Llorona jumped into the river, too, coming to her senses, realizing that she'd drowned her own children, her own flesh and blood, in the river. She searched the waters for them, but they weren't there. They'd been washed away and were never found, and La Llorona went crazy with grief and guilt.

"They say that La Llorona has been condemned to walk the banks of rivers forever after, crying — *llorar*, to cry, to mourn — as she searches for other people's children to throw in, to drown in exchange for the souls of her own children. She's cursed. Barred entry to heaven for eternity. They say she walks the banks of the river with the head of a horse and the body of a woman, seaweed dripping off her. If you see her, someone close to you will drown.

"But of course," Uncle Morrie would always add, trying to lighten the mood, "it's just a fairy tale told to scare little children into staying away from water. She's not real. You know that, yes? You don't have to worry. She can't do anything to hurt you."

Unless you were a three-year-old boy from La Paz.

In the first couple of months after moving to Australia, Rafi continued to worry that she was next on La Llorona's list — that La Llorona had taken a liking to her family, and it was only a matter of time before she came looking for Rafi.

As she listened to Uncle Morrie tell her the story, she would tick off the boxes inside her head. No horses nearby. Tick. No water. Tick. Well, there was the Yarra River, but Rafi didn't go anywhere near it. Never went in pools, never went to the bayside beaches, never went anywhere wet.

One afternoon, Uncle Morrie came over, set Rafi up at the kitchen table with her textas and a pad of paper and told her to draw him something beautiful. Then he went into the lounge room and quietly started talking to Rafi's mum.

"It was an accident," Rafi heard him say. "Just plain old bad luck. It's not healthy, Stel, telling Rif Raf that La Llorona did it. All this talk. She's always asking me to tell her the story. And I'm worried about you, Stel. If that's what you really believe, it's ..."

He didn't finish the sentence, but even at eight years old, Rafi knew what he meant. It was crazy, nutty.

"You think I should forget about him," Rafi's mum said, the temperature of her voice dropping to icy-cold.

Rafi wanted to go in and warn Uncle Morrie. Distract him, stop the conversation. She looked down at her drawing. It wasn't quite ready, but maybe it was enough to go into the lounge room with. Enough to entice Uncle Morrie away.

"How can I do that?" she heard her mother say, voice rising. "Forget about him? What sort of mother would I be? Act like he meant nothing? It hasn't even been a year, Moritz."

Rafi paused in the doorway to the lounge room, her unfinished picture wilting in her hand like a cut flower without water.

30

"Of course you shouldn't forget him. I'm not saying that."
Uncle Morrie's voice was placating, his hands up like a police-
man stopping traffic. "It's the worst thing that could possibly
happen to a mother. I know that. All I'm saying is, you need
to try to move on."

"I have moved on," her mum spat, the Spanish words
growling inside her mouth. "I've moved all the way out to
Australia to *move on*, as you say. But I will never forget him.
You don't have children. You don't understand."

"I've got Rif Raf," he said.

"It's not the same." Rafi's mum's voice dropped to a hushed
reverence. "You'd have loved Tonio."

"I did love him!" Uncle Morrie said. "I spent that week
with you over in La Paz. Remember? Of course I loved him.
Like I love Rif Raf. But she's here, Stel. Instead of always
looking backwards for Tonio, look at who you've got right
in front of you. She lost a brother, you know. And Ferdi. She
lost so much that day. Sometimes I think she lost her mother
as well."

Even an eight-year-old could see that was the wrong thing
to say.

The explosion had been swift and loud, a dam wall breaking. Words smashed and battered against the walls, drowning
Uncle Morrie in vitriol, in fury. He was in over his head.

Her mum cut Uncle Morrie out of their lives for months
after that. Even now, Rafi could feel her insides squeeze like
an accordion, all the air pushed out of her lungs, when she
remembered thinking she might never be allowed to see him
again.

It took so long — too long — but slowly Uncle Morrie
was allowed to come back into their lives. And Rafi never

asked him to tell her the story of La Llorona again. Ever. Because at that moment in the lounge-room doorway when her mum's words had splashed against her chest and legs like a rogue wave, Rafi stopped believing in the story.

There wasn't really a crazy woman with a horse's head trying to drown little children. What happened to Tonio was an accident, like Uncle Morrie said. Tonio wandered over to the horse trough because it was hot. He wanted to cool down. Once he'd fallen into the curved half-barrel of the horses' water, he couldn't stand back up. And he drowned.

No horse-headed woman had lured him there.

He was just a little boy left alone for a few unguarded minutes.

It was as tragic and awful and banal and mundane as that.

As Rafi grew up, her mother seemed to resent her more and let go of Tonio less.

Whenever they saw a three-year-old boy on the street, her mum would search his face, as if trying to find Tonio somewhere inside of him. Or turn away as if dismayed by the life in him.

Children near water sent her mum into a frantic spiral best dealt with by continuing Rafi's tradition of never going to the beach or the pool.

Horses, it went without saying, were a no-go.

Rafi told herself that there was something nice about her mum grieving forever for Tonio. Never giving up on him — soaked, saturated with the memory of him. She told herself that a mother who never forgot her son must love her daughter just as passionately, even if she had trouble expressing it. Even if she seemed not terribly fond of her most of the time.

When Rafi's mum, for no reason at all, started painting La Llorona again a few months back, Rafi felt the familiar weight of Tonio's memory push down onto her chest. She pretended not to notice as the paintings piled up, papering the walls, littering the windowsills, taking up every inch of space.

But then, just as suddenly, two weeks ago her mum stopped. She put down her brushes and paints and didn't pick them back up again.

Thinking it through now, Rafi wondered. Had her mum finally painted La Llorona out of her system? Was she — was Rafi — finally free of the horse-headed woman?

Rafi looked down at page twenty-seven. Trigonometry. She needed to concentrate. She needed to be able to think about sin and cos and tan without having some made-up legend from Latin American mythology rattling at her elbow while the rain outside rattled at the windows.

She closed her maths book and stood up.

She walked around their tiny flat and picked up every single lined exercise-book page, the newspaper pages with crayon sketches, the flattened painted-on cardboard. She got the ones on the kitchen bench and on the kitchen table and above the fridge and on top of the television and piled up on the couch and on the coffee table and on the bookshelves and next to the heater and at the end of the hallway and inside the broom closet and the sodden ones on the bathroom floor and the ones resting on top of the washing machine.

Every single picture, Rafi picked up.

She stacked them in a towering pile on the kitchen table. Then she separated them out. The small paintings into one pile, the foolscap-sized ones into another, the bit-bigger-than-thats into a third pile. And, finally, the big flattened-cardboard-box paintings into the largest but squattest pile.

She got a ball of twine out of the kitchen drawer and tied each pile lengthwise, then widthwise, until she had four piles of secured paintings. She put them beside the front door — smallest on top, flattened cardboard on the bottom.

She took every single Minties sculpture — all thirteen of them — off the windowsill and put them in a shoebox. She took the plasticine figurines and clay sculptures and wrapped them up in newspaper. She took the papier-mâché horse head and supermarket-bagged it.

Then she put those beside the front door as well.

Ideally, she'd have taken the entire toxic lot down to the rubbish bin and stuffed them all in, ground them down with her foot, then put the lid back on the bin and never seen them again. But all those years back, when Ferdi had done that, it had made things worse. As the paintings were squashed into the rubbish, her mum painted more and more La Lloronas, until she'd disappeared entirely inside her own head.

Rafi would do it differently. She'd leave the paintings there. The papier-mâché head. The horse-headed sculptures. Everything stacked by the door in case her mum still wanted them around. Then slowly, slowly, she'd take them downstairs, one bundle at a time, and put them in the bin until La Llorona was no more.

Rafi went back into the kitchen, piled up her books and pens and formulae, grappled them under her arm and went downstairs into the weather.

Fast, furious sheets of rain dragged the winter sky right down to splash at Rafi's feet. It was strange to think that above all those clouds and all that rain was blue sky and sunshine.

Clothes were clipped to the Hills Hoist out in the back-yard. Baby clothes — all-in-one outfits that belonged to Joshie from next door, the legs and arms whipping around in the cold August tempest, the baby-shape of the clothes making it look like it was Joshie himself clipped to the line and being tossed by the storm.

Rafi turned and went through the back door, into the warmth of Uncle Morrie's bistro.

The Artist

Dipper's fingers looked like they'd been left to soak in a box of Cheezels. But it wasn't Cheezels that had colored them Chinese-lacquer-yellow. It was ciggies. A daisy chain of ciggies circling from Dipper's mouth to ashtray, mouth to ashtray. Two, maybe three packs a day, seven days a week, for two weeks solid.

It took commitment to smoke that many durries, and Dipper was clearly the man for the job.

"We've made our point," Dipper said to Luke, pulling another fag out of his pack and whacking it into the slot of his narrowed mouth, then scratching at the lighter to get a flame. "They've agreed to increase funding. What's the hold-up?"

Luke walked over to the fridge and got out a couple of beers. Shut the fridge door and stood for a moment looking at the rivulets of rain running down the outside of the studio windows.

"There's no hold-up," he said, dragging the ring-pulls off both beers and handing one to Dipper, keeping the other for himself. "We're just making them sweat a bit longer."

"Making me sweat a bit longer, more like," Dipper said. He took only the briefest moment to slurp his beer and have a drag of his ciggie before continuing. "So now Real's over in Adelaide, and suddenly it's all over the papers that some guy in Adelaide is being offered the painting for three hundred and sixty thousand grand? You don't think that's a pretty big coincidence? All the guys at work are saying the whole Cultural Terrorists thing was crap, and the theft was all about making a shitload of money."

"Real's over in Adelaide because he's got an exhibition that was organized ages ago," Luke said, taking a sip from his beer and trying to use every part of his body language to convey "relax" to Dipper. He dropped his shoulders back, leaned against the table, breathed slowly, lowered his voice.

What he really wanted to say was, *You're carrying on like a fucking chick, mate. Get over yourself.* But that wouldn't help to calm the guy down.

"Don't worry what the papers say," he said. Blasé. Unhurried. "They don't know jack shit. Everything's fine."

Dipper took another slug of his beer, his leg jiggling, his entire body a jangling, jarring mess of nerves. No wonder he was such a skinny fucker. All that energy he used tapping his knee and pulling at his lip and rubbing his hand over his face. Not to mention the continual chain of cigarettes — hand to mouth, hand to mouth — clutched between his Cheezel fingers.

"I'm telling you, it's gone on too long," Dipper said. Beer. "If we get caught with the painting now, we're fucked." Ciggie. "I mean, we were always going to be fucked if we got caught, but now we're really fucked. Everyone's turned against us. At first everyone thought it was a bit of a lark, but now people are sounding angry. And that burnt match in the last letter hasn't helped, I gotta say."

Beer ciggie beer. Ciggie.

Luke had to agree that the last ransom letter the Australian Cultural Terrorists sent to the newspapers — number two in the series — had been a little too melodramatic, without quite the same wit and whimsy of the first. And, yes, the burnt match alongside the threat that the painting was about to be torched had maybe been a tad aggressive.

"You're getting all wound up over something that doesn't matter," he replied, attempting to recalibrate Dipper's rising hysteria. Because that's what Luke was starting to think Dipper was — hysterical. "As soon as the painting's returned, everyone will forget that there even was a burnt match."

"The cops keep coming round to my studio." Dipper wasn't listening. "They're always there. They keep saying to me, *You're a struggling artist and you were the security guard on the night of the theft, and the Australian Cultural Terrorists want increased funding for struggling artists, and they used someone on the inside to get the painting out. You can understand why we think you might have something useful to tell us.* They keep asking me, over and over, to tell them what happened that night. They know I'm in on it. We have to give the painting back. Tonight. We'll grab it from Real's — while he's still in Adelaide — and drop it off at the nearest cop shop. Or a locker at Flinders Street Station. Or Spencer Street. Doesn't matter. Wherever. The point is, we need to give it back. Now."

"Mate, we can't just waltz into Real's house and take the painting when he's not there," Luke pointed out. "There's a little thing called breaking and entering. He's got alarms set up. Besides, it's not there."

Dipper's body stilled. "What do you mean? Where is it?"

Luke shrugged a shoulder. No big deal. "I moved it a little while ago. Don't worry about it."

"Where to?"

"To somewhere you don't need to know about," Luke replied.

Dipper's leg started jiggling so hard it looked like it was about to go skittering off by itself — a spinning top completely unattached to the rest of his body.

"Real's set us up," he muttered. "He's gonna sell it behind our backs, mark my words."

"How about this," Luke said, keeping his voice measured, his hands flattened out on his knees. "We go round to Real's tomorrow night, as soon as he's back from Adelaide. Ask him about these rumors." He paused, waited, letting the word *rumors* sink in. "Because that's all they are. It's just bullshit that's being spread around because nobody has a real lead. Three hundred grand, you say? I don't think so. It's a Picasso. If Real was going to sell it, he'd be wanting a hell of a lot more than three hundred grand for it. Although, split three ways, I wouldn't say no to a sly hundred grand in my pocket."

Dipper flicked a glance at Luke, then looked away. His body had quietened down again at the thought of a hundred thousand dollars. Each. In cash.

Luke could almost see Dipper's brain ticking over. You could buy an entire house in Prahran for a hundred grand and still have change left over for a beach house, if you were into that type of thing. Or a new car. A holiday. Go and live overseas. Whatever you were into, you could do it if you had a hundred grand in your wallet.

"That'd keep you warm at night," Luke prompted.

"You'd do it?" Dipper blurted out finally. "You'd keep the hundred thou if Real offered it to you?"

Luke frowned. "Are you kidding? Sure. Why not? It'd set you up for life."

Dipper fired up again. "It'd be dirty money. I wouldn't touch it with a ten-foot pole. The thought of a beautiful work of art like that being kept in some bourgeois pig's basement would do my head in. Besides, you make enough from your own art. You don't need a slice of Picasso's pie as well."

Luke fought the urge to punch something. Or, more to the point, someone.

Dipper really hadn't been a good choice of person to steal a world-famous painting with. He had too much of a guilty conscience. He was too Catholic. Too earnest.

"It's not like it's happening anyway," Luke said. "The painting isn't being sold. It's just a *rumor*. Don't worry about it. You're getting yourself all worked up over nothing."

Dipper hadn't been a good choice, but what else could Luke and Real have done? He'd been there when they first came up with the idea, so if they hadn't included him, he might have blabbed about what he knew, or at the very least started asking them questions. Also, he was a security guard at the gallery, so there had been advantages to using him.

The problem was, now he was freaking out and about ready to break. And Luke and Real couldn't afford for anyone — especially not Dipper, not at the moment — to find out what they were really up to.

Real Sartori was an older man. He could have been anywhere from his late forties to his early sixties. It was hard to tell.

40

He owned the Sartori Gallery on Chapel Street. Dyed his hair a verging-on-unnatural shade of black. Was a "confirmed bachelor," which in the circles Real mixed in was code for gay.

These three things Luke could say with certainty about Real Sartori. The rest … well, he couldn't possibly know.

People said Real was the son of South American diplomats. Or maybe Spanish.

That he'd grown up eating every meal off Meissen china and sterling-silver cutlery, dished up by servants wearing white gloves and black-tie suits.

That his family was extremely rich. That his family was extraordinarily poor.

That he came from a large family. That he was an orphan.

That he left Colombia because he was gay. That he left Colombia because of his art. That he never set foot in Colombia in his life.

That he spent the sixties partying with Ali MacGraw and Steve McQueen and Yves Saint Laurent and William Burroughs in LA. Hanging out with Andy Warhol and Patti Smith and Robert Mapplethorpe in New York. Getting stoned with Talitha and Paul Getty, and the Rolling Stones and Prince Dado Ruspoli in Marrakesh.

That he discovered Jean-Michel Basquiat.

That he'd left New York before Jean-Michel Basquiat was even on the scene.

That he spent time in jail in Marrakesh for fraud.

That he moved to Melbourne because a very big, very angry Texan discovered he'd been sold a flashy expensive fake and wanted Real's guts for garters.

That he'd made his fortune forging Monets and Modiglianis.

41

That Real wasn't his real name, but Sartori was.

That it was ironic he called himself Real, when rumors abounded that some of the paintings he sold weren't.

Real had much-talked-about openings at his gallery and much-whispered-about parties at his home.

People said Real was having a fling with one of Melbourne's richest, most prominent businessmen. One of Melbourne's richest, most prominent *married* businessmen.

But it was all speculation. No one knew for sure.

Although there was one other thing Luke knew about Real.

He knew that stealing the Picasso from the National Gallery had been all Real's idea.

Melbourne's art scene was very small and difficult to break into, and it was generally only the well-established older artists who had exhibitions and made any money out of their art. The "names" rich people "invested in."

Younger artists had to make do, scrounging money off their parents or living on the dole, squatting in abandoned buildings, spending all their coin on materials until their star went on the rise.

However, in Melbourne there was one exception to this rule.

And that one exception was Luke Watson. Aka the next big thing.

Luke was only twenty-one years old when he first started making thousands out of every painting he sold. He was twenty-seven now, and whenever he held an exhibition, each of his paintings would have a red dot beside it before the opening had even officially launched.

He was the youngest artist ever to be bought by the Tate Gallery in London. His paintings were in every major collection in Australia. His reputation was formidable.

He was the one to watch. The one to buy.

And then there was Dipper. Guilt-stained, nicotine-stained Dipper. Every bit as talented as Luke. Worked just as hard. And got sweet FA for his efforts. No exhibitions, no funding, no reputation and no sales. He had to get himself a job as a security guard at the National Gallery a couple of years back because he wasn't making anything out of his art.

Dipper cared too much. That was his problem. He didn't have enough of the fuck-its about him. He wanted people to like his work. To buy his work. It was very important to him.

Whereas Luke couldn't give a rat's arse. He had the fuck-its in spades. Fuck it if they couldn't take a joke. Fuck it if they found his work offensive. Fuck it if they didn't buy it.

And the punters couldn't get enough of him.

Everything he produced, they wanted. And they paid a lot of money for the privilege.

His last exhibition had been based on Peter Greenaway's film *A Zed and Two Noughts* from the year before. He'd called it *Zed and Two Capitalist Pigs*: a series of gigantically oversized twenty- and fifty-dollar notes, each one with a different society dame in place of the portraits of Kingsford Smith and Howard Florey.

Flies buzzed and maggots squirmed across the bills.

It was an insult.

A fuck-you.

Luke publicly called it "A meditation on the fact that people who buy art are like maggots, feeding off the backs

43

of artists around the world, only buying something for the *investment value* they think it's worth."

And still the paintings sold.

The fuck-its. He had them in spades.

Everyone wanted a piece of Luke Watson. They didn't care if he insulted them or slept with them, as long as they got a piece of him.

And, generally, Luke Watson was happy to oblige.

Which was probably why he and his girlfriend had split up a few months back.

Well, that and the fact that one day he turned around and noticed she wasn't his type anymore. That she'd become possessive and clingy and boring, and he just wasn't into her.

Sure, having a baby probably had something to do with it, but regardless, she'd become a drag and they split up. End of story.

But also, ironically, start of story. Because when Penny, his ex, found a flat in Richmond to move into, it happened, co-incidentally, to be a flat that Real Sartori owned. And the day Luke and Dipper helped her shift her stuff into her new place, they ran into Real as they were coming downstairs to grab one more load of her shit.

Real had been meeting someone for lunch at the bistro downstairs from Penny's flat — which his brother ran, apparently. (Add that to the list of things Luke knew about Real. His brother lived in Melbourne.)

Real and Luke knew each other a little, had crossed paths at various exhibitions. So after shifting his ex's shit into her flat, Real, Luke and Dipper spent the rest of that afternoon in St. Moritz — that was what the bistro downstairs was called — drinking beers and throwing back tequila, stewing in cigarette and cigar smoke and getting drunker and more belligerent as the afternoon wore on.

"So in the meantime" — Luke had jabbed his finger at no one in particular — "people are off stealing cars and breaking into houses because priority number one of this fuck-knuckle government is to get the cops to clean up the *graffiti problem*. It's bullshit."

"It's the broken-window theory," Real said through the haze of smoke, leaning back in his chair as if he was taking command of the table. Which, in hindsight, it turned out that he was. "This is what it is. They started fixing them — the windows, in New York, neighborhood by neighborhood, all the windows — and crime levels dropped dramatically. Fixing broken windows and painting over graffiti stopped crime in its tracks."

"What? So if I do a bit of graff somewhere," Luke said, "which, by the way I'm somewhat partial to, then other people's dodgy deals are my fault? And if someone cleans off my work, crime stops? Just like that?" He clicked his fingers to make his point. "That's a lot of responsibility for one little tag."

"That's it exactly. Yes," Real said, smoothing out a crease on his pant leg. "Because this is what they worked out. If you paint graffiti, you're more likely to commit other crimes. That's how it is in New York. Our government, in its infinite wisdom, presumes this is how it will be in Melbourne, too."

And so it went on, the conversation swirling and tumbling and drifting and doubling back and distorting, all the while making perfect sense in the seamless way that drunken afternoon conversations seemed to have, until finally they landed on the subject of government funding for the arts, and how well and truly crap it was.

"Take Dipper here." Luke clapped Dipper buddy-buddy on the shoulder. "He's a shit-hot painter and should be able to spend his time painting, but instead he has to work as a security guard at the NGV because no one buys his work, because no gallery will exhibit it, because he isn't a *name*. But he can't become a *name* until he starts getting his art under people's noses. And then the government cuts arts funding and instead gives the money to people to clean up graffiti. Seriously, you can't possibly agree with it. Even with all your friends in high places, Real, you can't agree with it."

"The dole," Dipper interjected, swirling tequila around in his glass. "That's the extent of arts funding these days."

"Exactly," Luke said, pointing at Dipper. "It's bullshit."

Real was strangely sober, in that way that older men who could really sock their alcohol away seemed to have.

"You work as a security guard at the gallery?" he asked Dipper.

Dipper shrugged, a little defensive that he'd sold out. "Not making any money out of my art, am I?"

"You're right." Real leaned his elbows on the table. "That's a disgrace. You should be free to work on your art. You should do something about it," he said, a challenge in his voice. "Force the government's hand. Teach them a lesson."

He held a match up to his cigar and puffed out plumes of smoke like a steam engine.

"Take something that matters to them," he said thoughtfully. "Something they care about. Hold it hostage until they agree to your demands. Force them to increase arts funding. You two sit here babbling away, but talk does nothing. It is worth this much — *pfft*. Action is what counts."

"We should," Dipper mumbled, the tequila starting to make his tongue, his language, sloppy.

"A painting," Real went on. "You could steal a painting from the National Gallery. Hold it for ransom and refuse to give it back until the government increases arts funding. It would be easy for you," he said to Dipper. "You know the place from the inside out."

Dipper laughed. Drank more tequila.

"That new Picasso that McCaughey's so pleased with himself about," Real said, leaning forward and dropping his voice. "*The Weeping Woman.*"

It had seemed like a spur-of-the-moment idea thrown into a drunken late-afternoon conversation, but looking back on it — on the way Real had come up with the idea to steal *The Weeping Woman* just like that — Luke saw that it must have been on his mind for a while. That Real must have had the idea all along and been searching for the right people to execute it for him. Someone who had the necessary law-breaking gene. Someone who matched up with the broken-window theory doing the rounds in New York.

Someone who had a healthy dose of the fuck-its about him.

With a bonus security-guard buddy on the inside for good measure.

That afternoon they discussed, in theory, how they'd do it. The logistics of it. Was it possible? Could they get away with it? What about security? (Dipper snorted into his tequila. "You're looking at security right here. Me," he said, tapping his chest with his shot glass. "Security is the least of our worries.") When would be the best time to take the painting? What would their ransom demands be? What if they got caught?

The idea appealed to Luke's sense of anarchy. He liked the thought of protesting against niggardly government funding. It would be a noble gesture. A little something he could do in support of struggling artists — people like Dipper and their other mates who made zero money out of their art.

It was a bloody good idea. The perfect plan. And it went off without a hitch.

Until now.

Because now Dipper sat in Luke's studio, resistant to Luke's calming demeanor, to anything besides his own clamoring nerves, majorly stressed that things were going wrong.

"They're watching me," he said to Luke for the however-many-millionth time, wiping his mouth with a shaky hand. "The cops. They know I was involved. They can tell, and now they're watching me to see what I do next."

Just as Dipper shifted forward to stab yet another cigarette into the ashtray, there was a knock on the door. A heavy, pissed-off-sounding knock on the back door of Luke's studio. And Dipper looked like he was about to fold.

The Ex

Penny stood in the drenching rain with eight-month-old Joshie hooked neatly onto her hip like a belt loop. Her umbrella roofed both their heads in an attempt to keep them vaguely dry.

You'd think Luke would be able to answer his phone or return her calls. But, no. Apparently the only way she was going to have a conversation with him was if she came down to his studio and attempted it in person.

In the rain.

Conventional wisdom had it that it was a good thing to have at least one bastard ex-boyfriend in your past — a relationship you could look back on and think to yourself, *Thank God I'm not with him anymore. Dodged a bullet there.*

Key words? "In your past." "Not with him anymore."

Nowhere in conventional wisdom did you find the words, "Get pregnant and have his baby." Nowhere.

Or the phrase, "Stay in love with him even after you've broken up with him."

A Bastard Ex — a truly great Bastard Ex — managed to act like an arsehole at the same time as making you desperate for his approval. He made you hate him and adore him (with the scales tipping more toward adoration). He scored zero on the list of reasons to stay together, but topped the list of guys you most wanted to be with anyway. He made you jealous and angry and furious and humiliated and insecure and sullen and shy and clumsy and awkward and gawky and stupid.

With Luke, Penny became the worst possible version of herself. The type of girl she despised. Whingy, clingy, jealous. And madly in love.

Maybe that was why people called it "madly in love," because it required a degree of madness, of actual insanity, to remain in love with someone when all the evidence pointed to the fact that he was an arsehole and that you were better off without him.

Penny hugged Joshie close to her chest. She gave him a kiss on the top of the head. Sniffed at his hair, ran her mouth over his cheek.

She could hear music coming from inside the studio. Hunters & Collectors. Mark Seymour singing the chorus to "Say Goodbye," about not being made to feel like a woman anymore. Which was appropriate, because Luke didn't make Penny feel like she was a woman anymore, just like the song said. Although, perversely, he did make her feel more old-fashioned feminine than she'd ever felt in her life. Powerless. Submissive. Wench-like. Waiting to be rescued. By him. From him.

It was very un-PC.

Very un-women's lib.

Very intoxicating.

Bastard Exes had a way of making the world a very confusing place.

Penny had always considered herself a feminist. Of course she'd go to university like her brother. Of course she'd earn good money when she finished her journalism degree. Of course she was an independent, free-thinking, self-determining woman. This wasn't the 1950s. It was the 1980s.

And yet here she was, standing on the back doorstep, listening to Mark Seymour and thinking about how womanly Luke made her feel because he treated her like shit.

The first time she met Luke was at a pub in Parkville — Naughtons on Royal Parade.

She'd been crammed into a booth with a couple of guys from uni, Pat and Bill, drunk, the three of them skolling beers and showing off their favorite party tricks for scores out of ten.

Bill's party trick consisted of him turning his eyelids inside out, which was grotesque and funny and quite brilliant.

Ten out of ten.

Skol.

Pat's party trick required him to pop his shoulder out of its socket and let it dangle uselessly by his side — the legacy of a particularly rough game of footy.

Shades of *Dawn of the Dead*.

Ten out of ten.

Skol.

And Penny's party trick? It was a little something she'd perfected as a teenager growing up in the country.

She grabbed a steak knife from the bar, then splayed her hand out on the table and started stabbing idly between her fingers with the tip of the knife like a salty sailor. Slowly at first, carefully, tentatively, as if she'd never done it before. Not talking. Thumb, pointer, middle, ring, little, ring, middle, pointer, thumb, pointer, middle, ring, little ring middle pointer thumb pointer middle ring.

Then faster, more reckless, dangerous.

Thumbpointermiddleringlittleringmiddlepointerthumb-pointermiddleringlittleringmiddlepointerthumb.

There wasn't a single person in the bar who wasn't watching her, hoping she wouldn't stab herself, but also hoping she would. Waiting for the blood. As she went faster, the knife stabbed at the wood of the table, the motion of her hand became a blur, the silver of the blade flashed.

Pointermiddleringlittleringmiddlepointerthumbpointer-middleringlittleringmiddlepointerthumb.

And then she slowed down.

Thumb. Pointer. Middle. Ring. Little. Ring. Middle. Pointer. Thumb.

She raised an eyebrow at Bill and passed him the knife to see if he was game.

He wasn't.

Ten out of ten.

Skol.

When she went up to the bar later to grab them all another drink, Luke started talking to her.

He leaned an elbow on the bar and propped his chin in his hand as if he wanted to get a really good look at her. He asked her what she did. Was she at uni? What was she studying?

He wasn't particularly good-looking, but he had the most fantastic smile she'd ever seen — broad, wide, open, mocking. As if he knew something that no one else did. He looked like the sort of person everyone would want to be friends with.

They talked for hours that night.

She told him about growing up in the country, summer days spent swinging endlessly into the river. Nights at friends' houses finessing the knife game. How important it had seemed at fourteen, fifteen, sixteen, to get as good at it as she could. She told him about the freezing winter mornings in the country, riding her horse, sweat lathering like dishwashing suds on his flanks.

She told him that she'd moved to Melbourne a couple of years back to study journalism.

He told her about growing up in Papua New Guinea. About the Mudmen with their spears and helmet-faces. About how shit-scared he'd been of them. He told her about the local markets where he'd go shopping with his mum, picking vegetables out of cane baskets that had been plonked on the dirt. He told her about boarding in Queensland when he was a teenager.

About coming down to Melbourne so he could go to art school.

About the time one of his friends went crazy from too much dope-smoking and thought he was the new Messiah. For real.

At one point, Luke touched her face and said simply, "God, look at you." As if he couldn't quite believe her, couldn't quite believe his own luck.

He told her he needed to paint her.

Needed. A guy says a thing like that to a girl, he's going to hook her. Bad.

She went back with him to his studio.

It was hot, the beginning of March. One o'clock in the morning. Luke opened all the windows and left the back door ajar.

Down one wall was a long wooden table stacked with tubes of oil paint rolled up on themselves like colored snails with their homes on their backs. Jars of pristine blond bristle brushes of varying widths and lengths clustered at one end of the table — some as fine as only a couple of hairs, some as thick as what you'd paint your house with. Other jars had irregular sticks of charcoal poking out of them.

The floor was paint-spattered.

Horizontal windows ran the length of the building. Shafts from the streetlights illuminated the darkness. Along one wall were photos and other bits and pieces — random tickets from bands he'd been to see, a pair of X-ray gogs from a comic book, magazine pages stuck roughly to the wall with masking tape, postcards, Polaroids, photo-booth strips.

Paintings leaned against every wall, each of them different but with a definite look, a definite "style" to them. A style that, as she found out later, was very popular with art investors and galleries around the world.

Luke lit candles on the floor, on the table where his paints were, in empty wine bottles at Penny's feet. Penny sat on the couch and watched him move through the room slowly, as if he was stoned. As if he was moving through water.

He started picking through the charcoal sticks — first one, then another — and as he searched for the perfect piece, he said, not even looking at her, "I was thinking I'd like to paint you nude. You cool with that?"

He hadn't touched her, except for that moment in the pub when he put his hand to her cheek and said, "Look at you."

And now he was asking her to get her gear off. She didn't know if he wanted to sleep with her or paint her. Or both.

She felt her heart boom in that moment. Like ambos had put paddles straight onto her chest and plugged her into two hundred and forty watts. She wondered if that was what happened when you fell in love. If you only realized it had happened when your heart got an electrifying jolt.

She began to take off her clothes, as if she undressed in front of guys she'd only just met every day.

She unbuttoned her top button.

Her heart making a racket.

She unbuttoned the next button.

Her palms sweaty.

She unbuttoned the next button.

Her ears ringing.

She took a deep breath and unbuttoned the last button.

She shrugged the shirt off her shoulders and looked at him, but he was picking up brushes, testing bristles with his thumb, not noticing her half-undressedness. She unhooked her bra, hoping she looked good enough for him, hoping her boobs weren't too small. She reached around behind her and unzipped her skirt. Stood a moment and let it fall at her feet. Shucked her knickers off onto the floor along with the rest of her clothes.

Luke turned around and leaned back against the table, that piece of charcoal he'd been looking for in his hand, a brush pushed behind his ear like a hula-girl flower.

His eyes moved down her body. Slowly. He breathed deep.

"You okay?" he asked quietly, as if taken aback.

"How do you want me?" she asked.

He laughed. Gave that great smile. "I should paint you first."

She grinned.

In the half dark, she watched him watching her.

"You wanna lie down?" he asked her.

She lay down on the couch, still keeping her eyes on him.

He walked over to her. Ran his hands down her body. Him completely dressed. Her completely naked. He leaned down and kissed her, lay on top of her, his mouth tasting every bit of her as she lay there, her mouth devouring him. Starving hungry. She unbuttoned his jeans, impatient with the barrier his clothes were putting up, wanting to be with him, wanting to feel him in her hands.

"You're the coolest girl I've ever met," he whispered to her.

And look what he'd done to her.

Penny kicked at the base of the door.

It was raining. Seriously.

Just answer the door, bastard.

She bent down to Joshie's head and breathed in, filling herself with the smell of her baby.

Reminding herself of all the good things in her world.

Of course she wouldn't normally kick at a door, but that was the good thing about Luke's studio. It was an old office building in South Melbourne that was going to be knocked down soon to make way for the new freeway; a 1950s Communist-era building with gray carpet squares and offices divided by particle-board-and-glass partitions. Penny imagined it would have been an accounting firm before whoever it was who'd worked there shifted out of it and into (you'd have to hope) more comfortable premises.

You could kick the shit out of that door and nobody would care.

She wondered whether maybe Luke was on the toilet. Or maybe he couldn't hear her because the rain was so loud and the music was cranked up.

Then again, that's what she always did — made up excuses for him. He'd heard her knocking and was taking his good ol' time answering. That was more likely.

But he was definitely there. Mark Seymour told her so.

She could always use her key. She still had one — the key Luke gave her a couple of years back when he was still in love with her.

When she was special.

When she was his favorite.

"Use it any time," he'd said. And the way he'd looked at her, the grin that crinkled up his eyes as he brought her in close to him, the way he'd kissed her at that moment — well, it was one of the happy memories she still clung to.

Pathetic, really.

The last time Penny used her key to the studio was a few months ago when they were still living together. Before she and Joshie moved out of the house they'd shared with Luke.

Luke had a towel wrapped around his waist as he painted a girl.

Eighteen or nineteen years old, the girl had been. Maybe younger. Short choppy blonde hair, like Penny's. She was lying on the couch in the studio, laughing at something Luke was saying, her arms folded loosely across her body. An open, unguarded look on her face.

Naked.

A better version of Penny. A younger version. Sweet, pretty, funny, uncomplicated. Stomach flat. Legs great.

No baby.

Penny was only twenty-three years old, but seeing Luke painting that girl had made her feel ancient. Plain. Matronly.

She stood in the doorway gripping the handle of Joshie's pram, reminding herself through the palms of her hands that she was a mum now. That she wasn't able to sit for Luke anymore — even if he asked her — because she had a baby, and babies took up time, and so what if her body hadn't exactly sprung back into shape. She had a beautiful baby, and sometimes you had to sacrifice your body for your baby.

The girl had noticed Penny first. Said, "Oh," and then smirked, raising a conspiratorial eyebrow at Luke.

Luke glanced around at Penny. Didn't even bother taking his brush off the canvas, didn't come over to look in the pram at his little boy. Just glanced at her, then turned back to the girl. The naked nineteen-year-old.

"What are you doing here?" he said, his back toward Penny.

He drew a sensual curve on the canvas, following the form of the girl's waist, her hips, with his brush. He might as well have been running his hands down the length of her body, the way the brush followed the girl's contours.

"Who's she?" Penny said.

She heard her voice come out of her own mouth and regretted the way it sounded instantly. There was a tightness in the tone, a thin-lipped, pissed-off sound to it.

The girl giggled. Raised her eyes.

Penny felt heat flush her face — hot red humiliation like a cheap bar radiator. Fury bloomed and rushed from her cheeks down to her fists.

She let go of the handle of the pram and went over to the girl, grabbing her by the arm to drag her off the couch.

"Get out of here," Penny screamed, her worst self on full display — psycho, screeching. "Get out. He's got a kid. He's with me. Get out. Tell her to go!" She turned to Luke, who was standing by his easel watching her. Smiling.

He had a great smile.

He was like Frankenstein, proud of the monstrous version he'd created of her. It was the ultimate creative endeavor, Penny realized, to take a fully grown human and change them into the exact opposite of themselves, the worst version of themselves, by the sheer force of your personality.

It was like he thought he was God.

Some kind of Bastard God.

Luke opened the door. Finally.

"Hey," he said, frowning at her.

She wished she wasn't holding an umbrella.

Umbrellas were so dib dib dib dob dob dob. So fingers saluting at your forehead, Girl Guide, be prepared. *Oh, it's raining? No problem, because I've got my umbrella.* You're not worried you'll get wet, are you? *Why, no, because I've got my umbrella.* Be careful out there, it's pouring. *That's fine* — patting your handbag —*I've got my trusty umbrella.*

The very fact that you cared so much about getting wet seemed uncool.

"Hey there, little guy," Luke said, reaching out and grabbing Joshie from Penny's arms. "How you doing, mate?" He nuzzled Joshie with his nose. "You're getting so big."

And Penny fell in love all over again.

Seeing her little boy in his dad's arms, reaching up with his chubby hands to put his fingers in Luke's mouth, Luke pretending to bite down on them, as if he was going to eat them if Joshie wasn't careful. Of course she still loved him.

"So, anyway," she said, wishing he'd ask her in, wishing she could get out of the rain, wishing she could get out from under the dib dib dob-ness of the umbrella. "I left a couple of messages on your phone at home."

He continued looking at Joshie. Didn't even look up. It was as if he hadn't heard her.

It occurred to her that maybe he was stoned. His head was definitely somewhere else.

"I haven't been home the past couple of days," he said eventually.

She clicked her tongue, irritated by him. She could flick from love to irritation in an instant. That was the other thing with Bastard Exes. They left you completely unstable and wrong-footed.

"The thing is," she said. "I'm going out tomorrow night, and I need you to babysit Joshie for me."

Although, was it babysitting when Joshie was his kid, too? It wasn't like she'd created him all on her own. They weren't talking about the virgin birth here.

Luke looked away from her into the studio, then turned back toward her.

Someone was in the studio, Penny could tell. It would be a girl. A naked girl. Younger, prettier, better.

"I can't," he said. "I've got stuff on tomorrow night."

"I've got a date," she blurted, hoping that some spark, some spit of jealousy would ignite in him at the thought of her going out with another guy. Something to show he cared.

60

Or maybe she'd said it to be spiteful. To show him that she'd moved on, that she rarely gave him a moment's thought. That she simply needed him for babysitting purposes, because lah-di-dah, she had a date.

"Sorry," he said, handing Joshie back to her. "I'm a no-can-do this weekend. Get that kid next door to babysit."

"She babysits for me every Friday already, while I'm working," Penny said. "It'd cost me money to get her to do it Saturday as well."

"So don't go," he said. "Save yourself some bucks."

And he stepped back inside and shut the door on her.

The Guy

If Guy's mum was home, the house would look nothing like it did at that moment. The ashtrays would have been emptied, this afternoon's saucepans and dishes in the kitchen would have been washed and put away, the coffee table would have been wiped down, and the dishcloth would have been squeezed to near-dryness and put back in the cupboard under the sink.

If she was home. But she wasn't.

Instead, she was five hours away with Guy's dad and their friends, while in her place were Benj and Mish and Liv and a whole lot of lived-in slouchy comfortableness, which suited Guy perfectly.

There were beer cans (both the empty and the still-drinking-it kind) on the coffee table along with chip packets and full ashtrays and a mull bowl and dishes of semi-eaten 2 Minute Noodles.

The Breakfast Club was on the video player, with Molly Ringwald looking preppy and Ally Sheedy looking edgy and Judd Nelson looking sideways at Molly Ringwald and Emilio Estevez looking well pleased with himself and Anthony

Michael Hall looking like he was in totally the wrong movie because he looked so much younger than everyone else.

Liv sat on the floor, occasionally pulling her blonde hair up into a ponytail, occasionally dragging the elastic back out. Guy was on the comfy chair and Mish was on the couch, her feet up on Benj's lap already — a sure sign that tonight was going to be one of their fling nights. It happened occasionally, especially when they both let a few drinks lower their guard.

"So see here …" Guy said, rewinding the video back to the part where Anthony Michael Hall's dad is picking him up from detention. "That guy" — and he pointed at the screen — "is John Hughes. You know, who directed the movie."

"That right?" Mish said, her head perking up before lolling back against the arm of the couch. "So, is that the most boring fact you can come up with, or do you have more?"

"I got a million of 'em," Guy said. "And I'm storing them all up especially for you."

"Talking of parents, you just reminded me," Liv said, clicking her fingers and pointing at Guy. She pulled her hair back into a ponytail. "There's a note on the fridge that says your folks aren't getting back till Sunday night."

Guy looked at her. A scheme was written plainly across her face.

"So I'm thinking …" Liv said, grabbing a chip from the pack on the table but not putting it into her mouth because it might distract her. "While your olds are away …"

"*Yes!*" Mish said, sitting up as if she was a jack-in-the-box, *ba-doing*! "That's a brilliant idea."

Guy shook his head. "There's no way." He knew exactly what they were both thinking. "The olds'd kill me."

"But, Guy," Liv said, a lilt in her voice as she dipped her chin at him. "That's the deal. When the parents are away, the kids will play. It's like a foregone conclusion. An obligation. A commitment. Kids have been doing this since the beginning of time. Your parents would be disappointed if you didn't have a party."

Guy was pretty sure his folks wouldn't be disappointed if he didn't have a party.

"Promise me," his mum had said, tapping him on the chest before leaving for Mount Hotham, "that you won't have a party."

"Mum," Guy said, stepping back from her, trying to reclaim his personal space. "As if. I don't even want one. Besides, everyone's studying. I'm studying. I don't have time to party. If I had time to party, I'd come skiing."

"No party," she said, pointing her finger at him again. "I'm serious. When Liz and Andy went away last year, Steph had a huge one and their house was just about destroyed. It was a disaster. We're trusting you."

He remembered Steph's party. It had been excellent.

"I'm not going to have a party," he said to his mum. "Relax."

"Guy," Benj said, "I gotta go with Liv on this one. You're letting everyone down if you don't have a party. You're almost letting our entire generation down if you don't do it. You've got a responsibility to everyone our age to be irresponsible when your parents are away. Otherwise, what's the point in them going? They might as well have stayed in Melbourne."

"Just a few people," Liv added. "It'll be fun."

"They'll never know it happened," Mish added. "We'll leave the place perfect."

Guy took a thoughtful handful of chips out of the bag. He selected an extra-large chip from his palm and crunched down on it.

A party.

Him and a few mates.

A bunch of friends having a good time.

What was the worst that could happen?

The Girl

R afi walked into the bistro, her schoolbooks bundled under her arm.

"Rif Raf," Uncle Morrie said, looking up from the reservation book. "To what do I owe the pleasure?"

Rafi's hair was wet from the few short seconds she'd spent in the rain outside. She walked over and gave her uncle a smooch on the cheek.

He smelled nice. He always smelled nice. Smoky and toasty.

"Thought I might study down here," she said. "If that's okay with you. I'll be gone before people start coming for dinner. I'm babysitting soon anyway."

She didn't mention the fact that she didn't want to be upstairs when her mum came home from her cleaning job at the National Gallery, in case she went psycho at the sight of her paintings and sculptures and the crazy papier-mâché horse head all bagged up. The bistro seemed safer.

"You can stay as long as you like, Rif," he said, making a note in the margin of the bistro's large dinner bookings diary. "A pretty girl is always good for business." He winked.

Rafi plonked her books up on the bar and opened her maths book, checked her watch. It was 5:05 p.m. She had an hour before she was due to babysit. Fifty-five minutes, to be precise.

Uncle Morrie brought her a hot chocolate.

"Tell me," he said, resting his elbows on the bar. "How's it all coming along?" He nodded toward her books.

Rafi's schoolwork was the one thing in her life she had complete control over. The drafting and redrafting and re-drafting of her English essays. The rote learning of her maths formulae in the shower. The hour dedicated every night to memorizing the periodic table.

It was the simplest thing in the world, studying, as far as Rafi could tell.

Of course, some of the concepts — especially in maths — took a bit of figuring out before they'd sit straight in her brain. But she knew there was an order to it all, a reason for being. Study hard, get good marks — a very simple equation.

She'd sit at her desk or the kitchen table or in the flat next door while she babysat for hours on end and control the marks the teachers gave her.

So when Uncle Morrie asked how the studying was going, what he was really asking was, *You're not spending all your time studying? You're having fun?*

So different from her friend Frenchie's parents, who complained that she was going out too much. Rafi's uncles worried that she didn't go out enough.

"I've been going out," she said, raising an eyebrow at him. "I'm fine."

Fifty-three minutes later, Rafi gathered her books and went up to the flat next door.

"Fifi," Penny said, opening the door and grinning. She had a towel wrapped around her body and another one turbaned around her head. "You're early!"

She wasn't early. She was exactly on time. But Rafi's exactly-on-time often seemed to be Penny's you're-early.

No one called Rafi Fifi except Penny. She insisted that Joshie had been talking about Rafi when the first "fi" sound came out of his mouth in among all his other babbles, so Fifi it was.

"Hi," Rafi said. She held up her hand in a wave that struck her midway through as totally uncool, but she was there already and had to go with it.

Penny always made Rafi feel clumsy and awkward and schoolgirlish. It was something about Penny's cropped peroxide-blonde, rock-chick hair with the black regrowth. It was the Doc Martens — shoes, not boots — and the Levis 501s worn with a T-shirt, and the big dangly earrings.

Rafi stepped inside and looked around, marveling as she often did at how similar Penny's flat was to her own, but also how different. There was the same hallway, same two bedrooms off the hallway, same heater in the lounge room, same kitchen down the back — but with everything flipped and opposite.

Nappies were folded on the dining table. A clothes horse was in front of the heater, tiny socks and colored bras dangling off it.

A bottle of milk was ready on the arm of the couch.

The baby was tangled up in the telephone cord.

There was a warmth and hang-out comfiness in Penny and Joshie's flat that was the flip and opposite to Rafi's place.

Rafi put her books down in a neat pile on the dining table.

"Gimme a smooch, you crazy kid," she said, lifting Joshie up and plucking the telephone cord out of his plump-fingered hands, then wrapping him in her arms to suffocate him with kisses.

She sat down on the floor with him between her legs, then let him squirm away from her and commando-crawl on his stomach over to his mum, his entire body flexing first to the left, then to the right, then to the left again, feet pointing to the ceiling, worming his way across the floor, the chunk of his arms propelling him forward.

Rafi leaned over and squidged his chubster leg.

"You can't get away from me that fast, mister," she said, dragging him back for a hug. "Especially not with that wacky crawl thing you've got going on."

"Excus-ay moi," Penny said, picking Joshie up from where he sat plumped like a cushion in Rafi's arms and kissing him extravagantly all over his face. "Don't you listen" — *mwah* — "to a thing" — *mwah* — "that nasty Fifi says to you. Your crawling's" — *mwah* — "perfect. Besides, what would Fifi know? She's just" —*mwah* — "… how old are you?"

"Seventeen," Rafi said, grinning.

"See, she's only a kid. What would you expect" — *mwah* — "a seventeen-year-old kid" — *mwah* — "to know about the finer points of crawling?"

Rafi laughed and Penny put Joshie back in her arms. Rafi kissed his tummy, his fingers tangling in her hair, before she grabbed the bottle of milk off the arm of the couch and put it into his cherub mouth. He kept his eyes firmly on Rafi's face as he drank, as if he was studying her, memorizing her.

Babies were so ridiculously cute.

"So, Fifi," Penny said, pulling on her Doc Martens. "I have to go soon, but tell me quickly, how's the romance coming along?"

She said "romance" with a rolled r. *Rrromance.*

Rafi smiled.

Diff Cameron.

Diff. Breathe in.

Cameron. Breathe out.

Even his name was cute. It was as if his parents had gone, *What's the cutest name we can think of?* and come up with Diff Cameron. Well, David Cameron, but knowing that it would probably be shortened to Diff.

In Rafi's opinion, if you were asked to describe a Diff Cameron, Diff Cameron was exactly what you'd come up with. Blondy-brown hair, a bit long and flicky. Blue eyes with super-long eyelashes that were completely crushable all on their own. And he had this way of looking at you that made you feel like holding your breath, so not even a slight chest movement could ruin the moment.

"He's good," Rafi said. "I saw him a couple of weekends ago."

"And?"

A couple of weekends ago, Rafi and Diff Cameron had done that thing they sometimes did. That vaguely-talking-when-they-first-saw-each-other-then-not-talking-again-till-really-late-and-then-kissing-before-they-went-home thing they did. It happened sometimes. Not often enough for it to be a regular thing, but often enough for it to be a kind-of-regular thing.

Rafi wanted it to be a really-really-really-regular-every-weekend-with-calls-during-the-week type thing, but she wasn't sure exactly how to get there.

She'd done what she could to control the situation, but it still wasn't happening.

She listened to *Punter to Punter* every Saturday morning on 3RRR, so that she could keep up with footy news and talk about Collingwood whenever she ran into him.

She turned up at parties she'd heard he'd be at whenever she could.

She'd written "Rafi Cameron" — her married-to-Diff name — in all her school folders and textbooks hundreds of times, sometimes changing it to "Rafaela Cameron" for when she wanted to go formal.

She'd kissed him twelve times so far. (Thirteen, actually, but who wanted to admit to thirteen times when it was so unlucky? Rafi had decided she was going to keep it at twelve times until it was fourteen times, and skip thirteen altogether.)

She'd twisted apple stalks through their As, Bs and Cs, and it was surprising how often the stalk came away at D. Okay, maybe sometimes there was a bit of force used to pull the stalk out if it wasn't quite ready, but even with forced removal taken into account, it twisted off at D enough times for it to be significant.

And she'd spent a lot of time just generally thinking, *Diff*. Breathe in. *Cameron*. Breathe out.

"So, when do you see him again?" Penny asked.

"I don't know," Rafi said. "Soon. Hopefully."

Penny shook her head. "He wants to be careful or someone will steal you right from under his nose. Then he'll be sorry."

Rafi laughed. "Yeah. Doubt it."

"Talking of romance," Penny said, looking shy all of a sudden. "I've got a bit of a favor to ask. I've got a date tomorrow night. And I went to see my Bex" — Bex was what Penny called Joshie's dad, short for Bastard Ex — "to ask if he'd have Joshie, but of course, since he's an arsehole, he said no. So I totally understand if you can't, but … if you could baby-sit for me tomorrow night, too, that'd be great."

Rafi looked at Penny. She was blushing. Cool, sophisticated Penny, who could knock anyone out with a single glance, was blushing.

"I can do it," she said.

"It's probably not even a date, actually," Penny added randomly. "It's probably just a friend thing. I shouldn't have said date. It's just seeing a band. It's … it's a band thing."

"I can do it," Rafi repeated.

"Besides, I'm not even sure I want to go. I'd never even heard of this band until yesterday. And he's going with a whole bunch of friends, so I'm sure he'll be fine if I bail."

"Penny," Rafi said, not sure she'd been heard the first two times. "I can do it."

Penny looked as if she'd convinced herself that it wasn't a date and that maybe it wasn't worth going.

"Oh. But you might want to go out."

Rafi shook her head. "I've got nothing on. I'm happy to. It's just as easy to study at your place as it is at mine."

"You sure? I mean, I don't mind if I don't go. They're friends of … his. The band, I mean. They're friends of this guy. I don't even know them."

The way Penny had hesitated — the slight pause before she said "his" — made Rafi think maybe she knew him. She wondered with a jolt if it was maybe Uncle Morrie. He always seemed to spark up when Penny came into the bistro. And Uncle Morrie had plenty of friends who played in bands.

72

"So ..." Rafi said, tilting her head, "who's the not-date with? Anyone I know?"

Penny crossed her arms over her chest.

"You know Mick?" she said.

Rafi frowned. Not Uncle Morrie. Mick.

"Nope. Is he cute?" she asked.

Penny raised an eyebrow. "Not bad."

A flick switched in Rafi's brain. "Hang on a minute. Butcher boy?"

If it was that Mick, his family owned a continental meat business. His dad worked there, and his grandpa still worked in the office a couple of days a week. They delivered things to the bistro like blood pudding and brains and kidneys. Things Rafi wouldn't eat in a million years.

"Um," Penny said, looking a bit deflated by the description. "Well, yeah, I guess. I didn't know that's what people called him."

"No, I mean, that's what I call him. Sometimes. Actually, I don't even call him that normally. He's a spunk. You're going on a date with *him*?"

"It's not a date. It's a band thing."

It was a date. Rafi was sure.

Rafi officially met Penny for the first time a few months back, out by the clothesline.

Rafi had been helping her mum, and Penny came up, all smiles, and introduced herself, Joshie on one hip, basket of wet clothes on the other. She dropped the basket of clothes on the ground beside the clothesline and grinned at Rafi and her mum.

"Hi," she said. "I'm Penny. We've just moved in. This is Joshie." And she gave Joshie a quick kiss on the side of his head.

Rafi's mum made a thin-lipped attempt at a smile at Penny.

"I'm Estelle," she said. "This is my daughter, Rafaela. You have settled in?"

"Yes," Penny said. "It's great. Fantastic having a garden for Joshie. Our last place had nothing. Just a balcony. This is heaps better."

Rafi's mum settled her eyes coolly on Joshie, her mouth flat, cheeks sucked in. Then she looked back at Penny.

"Just you two?" she asked.

Penny's smile flagged for a moment before brightening back. "Yup. Just me and the little guy."

And she kissed him again on the side of his head, as if confirming that he really was hers to kiss as much as she wanted.

"I hope you like it here," Rafi's mum said.

Pegging the final shirt on the clothesline and turning to Rafi, she switched to Spanish. "You see? Young and pretty, but still no husband. It's like I've told you before. Men are bastards."

Rafi looked at Penny and knew there was only one word she'd understood in all of that. *Bastardos.*

Penny's smile dropped from her face. Rafi could see that she'd misunderstood. That she thought her mum was calling Joshie a bastard.

"That wasn't how it sounded," Rafi said to Penny.

But then she wasn't sure what else to say, because instead of apologizing, her mum shrugged and said to Rafi, "She doesn't know what I said, you stupid girl." Then she picked up the empty clothes basket and went back inside.

Estupida being the Spanish word that sounded most like its English equivalent in that sentence.

Bastardo and *estupida*.

Things were a little frosty at the clothesline after that.

One afternoon, downstairs in the bistro, Uncle Morrie started telling Rafi about the new girl upstairs. Penny.

"Oh, yeah," Rafi had said. "We met last week."

By the clothesline, where Mum called her stupid and her son a bastard, she didn't add.

"I mentioned you're quitting your shifts here, because you like nothing better than to leave your poor old uncle in the lurch." He winked at her. "And she said she might take them on, which would be great. But she needs to work out what she'd do with her little one."

The bastard, Rafi thought to herself wryly.

"She doesn't have any family in Melbourne. And it's not necessarily worth it for her to work here if all her pay ends up going to a babysitter."

Rafi hated the idea of giving up the money she earned waitressing, and she hated the idea of having to spend more nights at home with her mum than she had to, but she wanted to get into medicine next year. So she was giving up her shifts with Uncle Morrie because she'd decided every extra minute she could spend studying would be worth it.

Then again, she could study anywhere. She didn't need to be home to do that. And a little bit of extra money would be good. And she liked babies.

"Maybe …" she said, but then stopped.

Penny probably wouldn't want anything to do with her after that afternoon at the clothesline.

"What?" Uncle Morrie said, resting his elbows on the bar and concentrating on her. He brushed a strand of hair off her face so he could see her better.

"I was just thinking that I could babysit for her. And maybe once he went to sleep I could charge less or something. That way I still get a bit of money coming in while I'm studying, and she gets a bit of money from waitressing. And also, I get to have some time away from home, because if I'm not waitressing, I'll be at home a lot more, and you know."

Yes. Uncle Morrie knew.

He was her favorite, hands down. Where her mum was irritable, he was patient. Where her mum was tetchy, he would laugh. Where her mum was a bitch, he was whatever the complete opposite of a bitch was.

A bastard? Rafi thought to herself with a smile.

Uncle Morrie was the parent she didn't have.

"You babysit Joshie? That's a brilliant idea," he said. "I'll see what she thinks."

"It's hardly brilliant," Rafi said, raising an eyebrow.

"It's up there with splitting the atom and inventing penicillin as far as I'm concerned," he said, grinning. "She gets discounted babysitting, you get to study in peace, and I get someone to cover your shifts. It's what we call in the business a win-win."

"The only thing is," Rafi said, looking down at the bar, "she might not want me babysitting for her. Mum wasn't exactly Mrs. Friendly when we met last week."

"Don't even give it a second's thought," Uncle Morrie said. "Leave it to your old uncle to sort out."

The first time Rafi babysat, Penny was cool but not ice-cold. The second time, she thawed slightly.

The third time, Rafi said, "I'm sorry about my mum."

"Pardon?" Penny asked. As if she hadn't heard properly.

"You know," Rafi said. "The other week when we met. I mean, what she said probably sounded a lot worse than it really was."

Rafi couldn't quite bring herself to say "bastard" and "stupid" out loud. Not to Penny's face.

Penny didn't answer. She just watched Rafi.

"She's … I don't know," Rafi continued. "She wasn't talking about you. She was talking to me about something else completely different. Nothing to do with you."

Rafi knew she should stop. She'd addressed the elephant in the room, offered an apology, and now they could move on to some other topic of conversation. Talk about school, or how Penny was enjoying working for Uncle Morrie, or something about the weather. Anything that wasn't about Rafi's mum and that time a few weeks ago down by the clothesline.

"She usually speaks to me in Spanish," Rafi gabbed on instead, the words hurtling out of her mouth like a hundred-meter sprinter, "and I think half the time she doesn't even realize she's doing it. That other people might not understand what she's saying. Or that people might pick out a few of the words and think she's talking about them. Which she definitely wasn't. Not about you. She was definitely talking to me. About me."

Penny didn't say anything.

"Well, not about me exactly. I mean, she wasn't calling me a bastard." There. She'd gone and said it. And then her mouth was off again like a racehorse after the starting gun. "But she wasn't calling you one, either. Or Joshie, of course. I mean, as if she'd be calling him that. Because, I mean, he's not. He's cute as … and he's only a baby, but she was saying that men, you know, they're bastards. Which I don't even think is true, but that's what she reckons. And then when I saw you might think she'd meant Joshie … which you probably didn't even think, it's just that I worried you would … well, so then she called me stupid, but it might have looked like she meant *you* were stupid. Which she didn't. Because, yeah, she doesn't even know you, and so …" Rafi looked at Penny and stopped for a moment. "I'm making it worse, aren't I?"

Penny laughed. "Could be."

Rafi looked away.

"I'm kidding," Penny said, grinning. "It's fine. Men *are* bastards. Well, not all of them, but my ex certainly is."

"If she'd only explained to you what she'd said, it would have been fine," Rafi said, feeling the weight of her mum around her shoulders. "She does that sort of thing all the time. I'd almost think it was deliberate."

"I did think she was talking about Joshie. So thanks. And it's not that my ex is a total bastard. I don't want you to think that. Although he kind of is."

"If I didn't know better, I'd think she almost enjoys making people feel bad. Likes them thinking the worst."

"Schadenfreude," Penny said.

"What?"

"Schadenfreude," Penny repeated. "To delight in someone else's misfortune. Not that it's exactly schadenfreude, but kind of."

Rafi laughed. "Oh, that's my mum, all right. It's like she's waiting for something bad to happen to everyone, so she can feel that justice has been served or something. She's the ultimate Mrs. Schadenfreude."

Penny grinned. "Shouldn't that be Señora Schadenfreude?" she said. "Seeing as you're Spanish?"

"Probably," Rafi said. "Or maybe Frau would be better. Seeing as it's a German word."

Penny burst out laughing, and from then on the two of them referred to Rafi's mum as Frau.

Frau Schadenfreude.

Delighting in other people's misfortune.

The Artist

C reator and destroyer was what people called Picasso.
The ultimate bastard.

Cursed. Harbinger of doom.

Every art student knew the story.

When Picasso hooked up with Dora Maar — his muse for the *Weeping Woman* series — he already had a wife and a mistress.

He had two women, but he wanted a third. And Dora Maar was the cream of the crop.

She was a painter and a photographer — smart, fascinating, intense. The original femme fatale. She wasn't conventionally beautiful. Her eyes were hooded, her nose was long, her top lip was thin. But she had an interesting face — haughty, ice-cool. There was something of Greta Garbo about her.

Dora could hold her own in any conversation, with any of the intellectuals of her time. She was a muse to more famous men than Picasso. She hung out with André Breton, Man Ray and had an affair with Georges Bataille.

She was ubercool.

Picasso and Dora Maar became lovers and collaborated on his most famous, most celebrated work: *Guernica*. She was there with him constantly as he painted, photographing the enormous canvas as it changed and grew into the monstrous, violent indictment of the bombing of Guernica by forty-three German planes.

There was a photo taken of the two of them coming out of the sunlit water in Mougins, France, in which Dora looked like Ursula Andress (at a time before Ursula Andress had even signed up to become James Bond's cover girl) in a white bikini, her black shoulder-length hair slicked back with saltwater. Picasso walked beside her, a nuggety, balding, short little man, his bull-like shoulders and torso ever ready for a fight.

Both of them were so striking, in completely opposite ways. One yin. The other yang.

Picasso had met his match.

And then he set about systematically destroying her. Humiliating her. Making her feel small, unattractive, repulsive, even. One time he painted her with a dog's head. Another time he painted her as a lonesome flower-seller, people walking by ignoring her. (At this stage, Picasso was sleeping with his friend Paul Éluard's wife, Nusch, with Dora's reluctant agreement.)

He started painting his series of *Weeping Woman* portraits — Dora's face, hideously deformed and crumpling in on itself.

When asked why he had painted her like that, Picasso said that he was "just obeying a vision that forced itself on me. It was the deep reality, not the superficial one." That Dora, for him, was "always a weeping woman … and it's important, because women are suffering machines."

He told her, "You don't attract me. I don't love you."

He beat her up, leaving her unconscious on the floor.

He took a new lover, Françoise Gilot, who was twenty-two — forty years younger than Picasso. Fourteen years younger than Dora.

Dora had a nervous breakdown and had to be admitted to a psychiatric clinic for electroshock therapy.

She joined the oblates of the Order of Saint-Sulpice.

She became a basket case.

Picasso had cruelly and determinedly dismantled the human psyche of Dora Maar.

But Dora got a strange kind of revenge. In return for dismantling her humanity, Picasso started sensing that he himself had become cursed. That he, and those closest to him, were doomed.

A friend of his, an art dealer, came to have a look at Picasso's *Weeping Woman* series. On his way back to Paris, there was a car accident. The art dealer was decapitated by a bronze sculpture that had been sitting on the back ledge of his car.

Picasso's son was arrested for breaking into jewelry stores.

His mother died unexpectedly.

And as time went on, people started murmuring that his paintings were cursed as well.

"This version here," one of Luke's art teachers told the class years ago, holding up a copy of the most famous *Weeping Woman*, the one with buttercup yellows and vivid reds, "hangs in the Tate Gallery in London. The day it was first displayed, one of the staff who helped to hang it was knocked down by a taxicab outside the gallery and died.

"Another one" — he held up a painting of a crying boy — "was bought by a wealthy couple who hung it in their Paris apartment. Within a week, their apartment caught fire and was destroyed. The painting was saved, but nothing else survived.

"Picasso gave a rough freehand sketch to the daughter of the landlady of one of his villas, in Royan. The girl hung the painting on her bedroom wall, and that weekend her body turned up in the River Seine. Everything he touched was doomed."

Last year, in the months after the National Gallery of Victoria bought the acid-green and lurid-purple version of Picasso's *Weeping Woman*, rumors started spreading like oil in the waters of Melbourne.

It was said that one of the lawyers involved in the deal had a heart attack and died.

That one of the women who'd volunteered at the National Gallery had a grand mal seizure a week after the painting was hung and lost the power of speech completely.

That a security guard who worked at the gallery went home and found his son had committed suicide. That one was definitely true. It was one of Dipper's mates from work.

"Was that Penny?" Dipper asked when Luke shut the back door. Knowing full well it was Penny, as he could see the door clearly from his seat on the couch.

Luke nodded.

"How's she going?" Dipper asked. "I haven't seen her in ages."

Dipper had a secret crush on Penny, although it wasn't secret enough that Luke hadn't figured it out.

"She's okay. Penny's Penny." This explained everything, as far as Luke was concerned, about what annoyed him about her. "She wanted me to babysit tomorrow night. I said I couldn't. Because of, you know ..."

And Luke didn't say it, but what he meant was, *Because you want to go round to Real's place and sort out the painting.*

Dipper ran his hand over his face. "I guess we could go round to Real's on Sunday morning," he said, trying to accommodate Penny, figure out a way Luke could babysit. Which, by the way, Luke had about as much interest in doing as he had in returning the painting.

"It's fine," Luke said. "She's sorting something else out."

"It's just that if we don't give the painting back as soon as we can this weekend," Dipper said, standing up and pulling his car keys out of his pocket, "I'm worried that something bad is going to happen. That, you know, the curse ..."

Luke had to make a conscious effort to keep the disdain from showing on his face.

"Dipper," he said, short-temperedness creeping into his voice, "don't even go there."

Luke met Dipper nine years ago, when he first moved to Melbourne.

They met around the corner from art school, at a boxing gym Luke and some of his mates would go to.

Dipper wasn't like the beefcakes who pummeled boxing bags with arms like legs of ham. He was skinny, wiry, as if his skeleton was made up of bent-into-shape coathangers.

He was built for speed, not strength. When you got him into a ring with one of the bigger blokes, he'd spend the first few minutes ducking and weaving, tiring out the beefcake before landing a punch on their sweet spot and flooring them just like that.

He'd come to boxing classes for that classic reason of wanting to beef up, only to discover that his leanness, the very thing that had inspired him to sign up, was his advantage — the thing that kept him winning once he stepped into the ring.

Luke painted a series of portraits of Dipper for an art-school assignment, silk boxer shorts on, up against one or another of the Mike Tyson pretenders from the gym. Pretender toppled, Dipper victorious.

When Dipper heard that Luke didn't have family in Melbourne, he insisted that he come for dinner with his own family at least once a week.

"Can't imagine not having family around," Dipper said. "It must be shitful."

Luke didn't find it particularly shitful, but when he met Dipper's family he understood why Dipper would think so.

The Di Palmas were a cracking good family.

Mrs. Di P. would make multiple courses every night and not sit down at the table, instead piling people's plates with food, more food, always telling Luke to eat more, have more of the eggplant something, or maybe he'd like a bit more tomato whatever, have some pasta, he hadn't eaten enough salad, mop it up with the bread, he needed dessert. *Mangia, mangia, mangia!*

All that food every night, and Dipper was skinny as a tube, like the food just went straight through him.

There were always arguments over the dinner table, but funny, good-natured ones.

One night, Luke remembered, Dipper complained to his dad that whenever he went out he had to drive his mum's beaten-up old Datsun 120Y.

"I'll never get a girlfriend with that car," Dipper said, and his dad nodded.

"That's true," his dad said, folding his arms and resting them on top of his well-fed belly. "When I was looking for a car to buy your mamma, I thought to myself, *But Tony will need to drive this car as well*. So I looked long and hard, and I find the car outside, and I say to myself, *No self-respecting girl would be seen dead in a car like this*, so I decided that it was the perfect car for my boy."

And he laughed at his own joke, and Dipper laughed, too. Because Mr. Di P. was right. It was a shitbox of a car that no self-respecting girl would be caught dead in.

"So tomorrow," Dipper said, jiggling the keys to his mum's shitbox car in his hand and preparing to make the dash from the back door of Luke's studio through the rain to the car. "Yeah? We're giving the painting back tomorrow."

"Yeah, yeah," Luke said. "Tomorrow for sure."

Tomorrow, for sure, wasn't going to happen.

The Ex

Luke occupied too much of her headspace, Penny decided, as she tied her apron around her waist and went to the front bar to check out the reservations book for that night.

After all, it was a fairly safe bet that she didn't take up the equivalent amount of space in his head. She doubted he'd given her another second's thought after he handed Joshie back to her this afternoon and told her he couldn't babysit tomorrow night.

Five tables of four, seven tables for two, and one booking for twelve people. It was going to be a busy night.

Come to think of it, she should thank him for reminding her what a Bastard Ex he was. The way he'd said, *So don't go. Save your money.* Like the true bastard that he was.

Bastard.

She went into the office and took the key out of Moritz's desk, opened the safe and took out the change for the till.

Thank God she didn't live with Luke anymore. She was lucky to be in her own place, away from him.

It was good that they'd broken up.

She put the key back in Moritz's top drawer.

Which reminded her. She should give Luke back the key to his studio. She didn't need it anymore. She should drive past and drop it in his letter box tomorrow, make a statement.

But what if she needed it one day? What if he called her and asked her to go to the studio and pick something up for him? What if they got back together? It was just a stupid key, after all. It didn't mean anything. There was no symbolism in a crappy old door key. If she left it in his letter box it might seem like she was upset, pissed off, and she wasn't. She couldn't care less about him. She had a date tomorrow night, and Rafi was going to babysit Joshie, and she was getting on with her life.

Penny went out to the bar and separated the money into twos, fives, tens, twenties and fifties. Tipped the plastic bags of coins into their compartments in the till drawer.

She thought about the way Luke had cuddled Joshie when he first opened the door that afternoon. The way he nibbled on his fingers. The way Joshie's eyes stayed fixed on his dad's face, following every expression, every movement of Luke's mouth.

The way Penny's eyes had done the same thing.

Luke wasn't always a bastard. Not always.

She wouldn't return his key tomorrow. She'd keep it. Just in case.

Penny hadn't used the key or come to the studio for months. Not since that time, with the other girl.

That time, she stormed out without another word, pushed Joshie's pram fast all the way back to the place she shared with Luke. As she walked, she made a decision. She decided she wasn't going to be the worst version of herself anymore. Just like that, she would go back to the girl she had been before Luke, before Joshie. The one who was studying journalism at university. The cool one. The girl Luke had fallen in love with.

No wonder he wanted to paint other girls.

Grabbing at the girl's wrist, yelling at her to get out.

"Screaming like a banshee" was how her mum would have described it.

So the next afternoon, Penny pushed Joshie in his pram up Chapel Street, across the bridge over the Yarra with its upside-down muddy waters, into Richmond, and started traipsing the maze of streets behind Richmond Station, negotiating the narrow, pram-unfriendly footpaths, searching for a street called Cherry Tree Lane.

Simone, a girl Luke had gone to art school with (her paintings were beautiful — tiny blue, green and pink brushstrokes like Monet's, only set in skate parks and at outdoor concerts), had been living in a flat on Cherry Tree Lane in Richmond, but was moving to Sydney and had put the word out that it was up for grabs.

And Penny had decided to go grab it. The problem being that she didn't know exactly where Cherry Tree Lane was — just that it was apparently somewhere behind Richmond Station. Which would have been fine, except the entire suburb of Richmond had varying degrees of behindness to Richmond Station.

She tramped along, pushing Joshie's pram through the grid of Richmond. Every street had a similar industrial feel, with workmen's cottages and footpaths only just wide enough for a pram, and garage-type factories fronting right onto the street. She should have checked a Melways, but she hadn't realized how hard it would be to find.

But then she spotted it. Cherry Tree Lane, just off Cremorne Street.

"It's a great place," she remembered someone saying about Simone's flat. "Gorgeous art deco building with a bistro downstairs, so you don't even have to cook if you don't want to."

Down near the end of the street, Penny spotted a block of flats with a bistro underneath. Bingo. She walked to the bistro and pushed the pram through the door.

"I'm a friend of Simone's," she explained to the guy at the bar, which was kind of true. *I've met her once* seemed too convoluted. "She told me you're looking for someone to rent the flat upstairs."

Simone had told someone who'd mentioned it to Penny, but again — convoluted.

The guy gave Penny a key and sent her upstairs to the flat on the left, number two. It was exactly what she wanted. Two bedrooms — one large, one baby-sized. Freshly painted white walls, pretty ornate ceilings, polished wooden floorboards and a kitchen that was neither here nor there, just average. In the lounge room there was a little alcove overlooking the cherry tree in the front yard, perfect for a tiny dining table.

Penny told the guy behind the bar that she was interested.

"How many of you?" he asked.

"Just the two of us," she said. "Joshie and me." No Luke. No bastard, towel-wearing Luke.

"I'm Moritz," the man said, his voice gravelly, an accent barely noticeable. "Pleased to meet you. So, Simone's moving out next week. Does that work for you?"

"But don't I need to fill in some forms or something?"

Moritz shrugged. He took two cups down from the shelf and put them under the valves of the coffee machine.

"You can if you want," he said, picking up the doover and clicking some coffee grounds into it, then fitting it into position and pressing the hot-water button.

He put a cup of steaming coffee — black, no milk, just the way she didn't like it — on the bar between them and tipped the hot contents of his own cup down his throat.

"So, you want it?" he asked, plonking his cup down and resting both hands on the counter.

"Definitely," she said, picking up her cup.

"Done," he said.

She hadn't mentioned that she didn't have a job.

One thing at a time, as her mum always said. One thing at a time.

A few weeks later, having moved in and moved on from Luke (although not really), Penny was downstairs in the bistro having a coffee, Joshie asleep in his pram, the employment section of *The Age* spread out on the table in front of her and a red pen in her hand, ready to circle anything that looked remotely single-mother-friendly.

"I might be able to help you with that," Moritz said. "Do you waitress?"

"Um ... sure." She had never waitressed in her life. "When I lived back up in the country." *Bullshit, bullshit.*

Moritz smiled down at her and shrugged.

"Experience not necessary," he said.

"Oh. Well, in that case, no, never."

He laughed. "My niece wants to give up her shifts. She's in Year Twelve and needs to concentrate on her studies. She lives in the flat next door to you. You've met her?"

"She's your niece?" Penny said.

"Yeah," Moritz said. "Rafi is my niece. Her mum, Estelle, is my sister."

"Right."

Penny had met his niece, all right. And his sister. It hadn't been an introduction she was likely to forget in a hurry.

"So, this is just me running off at the mouth, but if you want a job, I need someone. Pretty much straight away."

He'd be in his late thirties, she figured, or maybe his early forties. His hair had streaks of gray through it, his eyes had laugh lines around them, and his whiskers had a faded livery about them that made him seem slightly weary — tired but relaxed.

He was cute for an old guy, Penny thought to herself, if you didn't mind the lived-in rumpled look.

"Of course you've got your little fella to consider, but the thing is"— he rubbed his hand over his mouth thoughtfully —"Rafi, my niece, well, she can pretty much study anywhere. In fact, she often likes to come down here and study at the bar, just for the company. So maybe Rif Raf — Rafi — could babysit your little guy while you're working. It could be a good little arrangement."

Penny chewed on her thumb.

"I'm not sure she'd be interested," she said finally, remembering what her mum had said at the clothesline.

"I'll talk to her. But if she's up for it, you're in?"

Penny's money situation was so dire she felt like she was drowning. There were bills. There was rent. And there was a whole lot of nothing coming her way from Luke. Being a single mum was hideously expensive, as it had turned out.

Penny held out her hand. "I'm in."

And they shook on it.

"I happened to bump into Simone," Penny told Luke back when she put her moving-out on the table. "She mentioned something about her flat being up for rent, and it kind of went from there."

This was a lie. She had purposefully walked the streets, hunted down the flat and set her mind on moving in.

"I feel like maybe we could see how it goes living in different places for a while because, you know, everything's happened so quickly. Joshie, living together ..." *Okay, so not everything, just those two things.* "And we've been annoying each other lately ..." *You're sleeping with other girls, and I'm the worst version of myself.* "And maybe if I move out, we can put the romance back into our relationship."

He didn't argue with her. Instead, he helped her move her stuff out. And hadn't given her a cent since.

Every now and again he'd throw in a *You're the one who wanted a baby, not me,* and she'd feel like there was nothing she could say in response.

She tried not to cry in front of him, but sometimes it was impossible. She'd weep from frustration at how impossible it was to get him to help her.

On the other hand, Penny's entire flat was decorated with beautiful paintings he'd given her. Thousands and thousands and thousands of dollars' worth of art. She could sell one piece and it would cover her rent for the entire year.

But she didn't want to sell his art, because each painting belonged to Joshie. She was only the caretaker.

Not to mention that she'd have to go through Luke's dealer for the proper paperwork — provenance, it was called. Then Luke would hear about it, and there was every chance he would never give her any of his work again.

And she needed it. She needed his paintings as a nest egg for Joshie. And she needed them because she liked the fact that sometimes he would turn up at the flat with a painting under his arm or a sculpture in his hand and say, *I thought you might like this*, or, *I made this and thought of you.*

She needed those moments. They were small and pitiful, but they were the only nuggets he gave her these days.

Just a week ago he showed up with something he thought she might like. A copy he'd painted of the recently stolen *Weeping Woman*, all neon greens and clashy purples.

"Actually, there's lots wrong with it," he said when she commented on how good it was, how much it looked like the one on the front page of *The Age*. "The colors are a bit off, and it's a lot smaller than the real thing, obviously, but, yeah, it's not a bad version. There's this exhibition coming up in Sydney in a few weeks, of a bunch of different copies. This is my version. So I'll need to get it back off you later, but for now I thought you might like it. Not everyone has a Picasso on their mantelpiece. Even if it *is* a fake."

It was the little things like that. Little things that meant a lot.

She faithfully hung each piece he brought over on the walls of her flat, or put them on the mantelpiece above the heater, or on the kitchen bench, or on the windowsill in the bathroom or the wall of her bedroom or her dressing table or in Joshie's room.

She saw him when he felt like it and not otherwise.

And she tried to move on with her life. Unsuccessfully.

The good news was that waitressing was fun. The other girls were great. The chef was scary, but Penny could generally avoid him. And Moritz was a sweetheart — friendly, relaxed, generous. Hospitable.

It was a pleasure to watch him with Fifi. He adored her — clearly thought she was the prettiest, cleverest, most adorable seventeen-year-old he'd ever met.

Which, in fact, she was. Penny was surprised at what good friends she and Rafi had become.

Penny was unsure at first. Reserved. After what Frau had said that afternoon at the clothesline, she decided it was a case of like mother like daughter — and tarred Rafi with the same brush.

But in fact they were polar opposites. Frau Schadenfreude was … Frau. She would look at Penny with a downturned mouth, or she'd ignore Joshie as if he wasn't a real live person worthy of at least a minimal hello, and it was hard to feel anything but irritated by her.

One night, though, Moritz told Penny about his sister — about her little boy who'd drowned. About the La Llorona legend that she blamed for his death.

After that, whenever Penny thought about little Tonio being lifted out of the horse trough back in La Paz, she felt a wash of sympathy for Frau.

And there were times when Frau seemed concerned about Joshie — almost kind, although even in these moments she'd manage to put a snappish edge in her voice.

For example, only this week as Penny and Joshie were coming back from the park, they ran into Frau, who looked in the pram and smiled at Joshie (if you could call it a smile), then told Penny to keep him away from water.

"Babies drown," she said, her Spanish accent evident in all her words. "Even if not much water, they can drown."

Penny said, "Oh, I'd never let anything happen to him," and as she said it she wanted to grab the words back, put them back inside her mouth, because she realized how it sounded. Like she thought only a careless parent let something bad happen to their children. Something bad like drowning.

She watched Frau's face close up on a fury looming beneath the surface that was so large, Penny felt sure it would have knocked her off her feet if Frau had unleashed it.

She wanted to tell Frau she didn't mean it. That what she meant was she'd always keep an eye on Joshie around water. She wanted to thank Frau for warning her. But Frau stalked away before she had a chance.

LETTERS TO THE EDITOR
August 16, 1986

Foreign extravagance
$1.6 million for something a foreigner has daubed? I don't care who he is. If our near-bankrupt government gives more money to these whiny art people it will be a shameful disgrace.

William O'Malley, Box Hill

1986 or 1906?
Are *The Age* Access contributors (6/8) living in 1986 or 1906? Picasso's masterpiece is about the anguish and despair that follows a horrific wartime event. It is an expression of a human's feelings. Melbourne, you embarrass yourself with your ignorant opinions.

Joan Reidel, Prahran

Tired old jokes
Picasso was original, unlike the tired old jokes about children being able to do better.

Eric Hanover, Northcote

The Party

The Girl

There was a simple technique for cutting hair when you didn't have a clue what you were doing. Instead of cutting horizontally across the hair (which ended up accentuating every line you cut), you pointed the tips of the scissors toward the scalp and nipped like a little sparrow taking worms out of the ground, each cut difficult to spot in among all the other snippy cuts.

At least, that was the technique Rafi had developed over the past few months. It was the one that worked best for her.

Paul Kelly was on the stereo, "Before Too Long" wending its way from the speakers in the front room down the hallway to the bathroom, where Joshie sat on Penny's knee, his hands palm up as he tried to catch his mum's falling hair with each chop — a little game he liked to play whenever Rafi cut Penny's hair. Blunt clips of Penny's peroxide-blonde hair drifted past his hands onto the tiled floor like furred autumn leaves.

The first time Penny persuaded her to take up the scissors and "hack away," Rafi felt as tense as an overblown balloon, all thin-skinned and with breath held until she finished.

Penny didn't fully understand exactly how neat Rafi liked things — the straight lines she preferred, the place for everything and everything in its place. Penny had never been in Rafi's flat, so she'd never seen her bedroom — the bed made to perfection, the sheets stretched tight over the mattress so that not a single crease could survive. Penny didn't know that Rafi's bookshelves were color-coded. That her jumpers were folded in that way they did it in shops. That all her drawers were lined with paper and then divided into neat sections with cardboard, which Rafi had cut using a scalpel, her ruler and a drafting triangle.

It went without saying that Rafi was not the type of girl who felt comfortable cutting another person's hair without knowing exactly what she was doing.

But somehow Penny managed to convince her, and Rafi found that she actually enjoyed doing it.

As she snipped, she would feel her shoulders dropping, her jaw unclenching. When she was in Penny's flat, she felt like maybe the world could be the sort of place where a girl could make mistakes and it wouldn't matter. A place where mistakes were celebrated, even.

After Rafi put down her scissors, Penny would look in the mirror, first this way, then that, then put her arm around Rafi's shoulders and say she loved it, that it was perfect, that Rafi was a natural, that it was exactly what she'd wanted …

Then she'd rub some gel between her fingertips and spike it up so that it looked even more messy and choppy.

And the craziest thing of all was that people apparently asked Penny all the time who cut her hair (although Rafi suspected it was more the girl under the haircut rather than the haircut itself that got all the attention).

"I tell them they wouldn't be able to afford you," Penny would tell Rafi. "I tell them that you're very exclusive and very selective about whose hair you cut. Which is true, because you only cut mine."

Tonight, Rafi had to admit she'd done a particularly good job on Penny's hair. It was like the love child of Annie Lennox and Grace Jones — black and blonde and spiked all over.

Which was, apparently, exactly the look Penny was after.

"I can do yours next if you'd like," Penny said to their reflections, picking up a thick hank of Rafi's long dark hair and holding it up to the mirror. "Give you a whole new look."

Rafi grinned at Penny and shook her head.

"You've got the perfect face for short hair," Penny went on. "It'd make your mouth stand out even more than it does already."

"But I might not like it."

Rafi remembered the disaster of Sophie-at-school's perm a couple of years back. Who could forget it? She came to school with a hat on and refused to take it off for the entire day. By the time she relented and showed them what her hair actually looked like, she had a bad case of hat-hair on top of these crazy curls that were insanely out of place in her previously straight hair.

"Wouldn't matter," Penny said. "It'd grow back. That's the great thing about hair. It grows."

Penny didn't seem to realize how wrong things could go. If things — hair, life — got too choppy, Penny simply adapted to the new look. Spiked up, dressed down — whatever it took to work with the new format. Whereas Rafi knew that some things couldn't be fixed simply with hair gel and a backcomb.

"So can I?" Penny asked, taking the hair-covered towel off her shoulders and putting it in the laundry basket, then turning back to Rafi. "Cut your hair tomorrow?"

Rafi pretended to give the matter some thought — tilted her head, eyes toward the ceiling, finger on chin — then shook her head.

"Nuh," she said.

"Scared?" Penny said, turning the taps on to fill Joshie's bath.

"Of you and scissors? Yeah. Definitely."

"What about this?" Penny asked, hauling a man's white dinner shirt out of her wardrobe and putting it on over her jeans — the lace of her bra visible at the spot where the buttons unbuttoned, dangly earrings dangling — then throwing a man's dinner-suit jacket with a brooch of an airplane on the lapel over the top.

She had no makeup on (or not so you'd notice), except for a slash of red lipstick that made her look like an overexposed photograph of herself, all mouth and short peroxide hair.

"That looks divine," Rafi said, sitting cross-legged on the bed and keeping half an eye on Joshie, who lay sleepily in her lap winding her hair around his plump fingers.

Every time she babysat, she fell a little bit more in love with him. He was so smooth and soft, like a velour-covered baby. And the way he always gripped her hair when he felt sleepy nearly broke her heart. Too, too cute.

Rafi wondered how old she'd be when she had her first baby. Wondered whether she'd stay with the dad or not. This could be her in a couple of years' time — baby on her lap, just broken up with her artist boyfriend, living in a flat of her own, about to go on a date with some new guy she'd just met.

Although that would mean she'd have broken up with Diff, which would be bad. If she was going to have a baby with Diff, she wanted to be with him forever.

Maybe she wasn't with Diff yet, though. Maybe their future was about to start. Maybe she'd accidentally had a baby with some other guy, and she was going to see the band tonight with Diff, and it had been so long since they'd seen each other but they still had all these feelings for each other …

Sometimes Rafi could hardly wait for her life to begin.

Penny looked at herself in her bedroom mirror, tipping her head, turning to see how she looked from the back, as if checking herself out from each angle would make a difference to her decision.

"Too formal," she decided.

She pulled the jacket off, shrugged the white shirt back over her head and started rifling through her drawers looking for the exact right thing.

"I don't want Mick to think I'm trying too hard."

She took out a different white shirt — a bit more fitted but with padded shoulders and a Peter Pan collar — then ditched the jeans and put a gray-blue fitted pinafore dress over the top instead. She grabbed a beret from her wardrobe and turned to face Rafi.

"Verdict?"

"Gorgeous," Rafi said.

"Band-appropriate?"

It was a revelation for Rafi to watch Penny getting dressed. She always looked like she'd grabbed the closest coathanger and tossed whatever was on it onto herself, then grabbed the second-closest coathanger and tossed whatever was on that onto herself, before grabbing the first pair of shoes and the first pair of earrings and the first necklace and the first few bracelets and heading out into the world.

Thrown together.

Looking gorgeous.

But now here she was, picking things up, holding them against herself, looking to Rafi for advice.

She didn't throw it together. She thought about it. Then she threw it together.

"Definitely band-appropriate," Rafi said.

Not that she went to see bands all that often. In fact, ever. She'd got to be in the audience of *Countdown* a couple of times through Frenchie's dad (who was a producer or something, Rafi wasn't exactly sure what). But bands in pubs? No.

Penny pulled the pinafore dress and shirt off and put the beret back on top of the wardrobe.

"I think I'll just go normal," she said, pulling on a loose floral dress, then grabbing a handful of necklaces and chains and putting them over her head. She added gigantic dangly earrings, hauled out the man's dinner jacket for the second time. Pulled on thick black tights and Doc Marten shoes.

Gorgeous. She was thrown together and gorgeous.

Penny leaned down and gave Joshie a kiss.

"Almost time to go, mate. Are you going to be good for Fifi?"

"Is Mick picking you up?" Rafi asked.

"Nuh, I didn't want him coming here," Penny said. "Too much single-mother business going on, you know. Babysitter, baby, bottles of milk. That type of thing.'

Suddenly Penny stopped, tilted her head like a bird checking for predators, said, "Oh shit," and ran from the room.

Rafi looked at the empty space where Penny had been, wondering what the hell. Then she picked up Joshie and followed her, realizing as she did so why Penny had run out.

The bath. The bath they'd been filling for Joshie.

It had overflowed to the God-damn.

An hour later Rafi was sitting on the floor leaning against the couch, her school books spread out in a semicircle around her, the stereo turned down to whisper-quiet so she didn't wake the newly fast-asleep Joshie as she listened to the Violent Femmes.

She'd heard of the Violent Femmes before, of course — knew they were considered majorly cool — but she hadn't been exactly sure what they sang until she spotted the record in Penny's collection tonight and put it on. As it turned out, she knew their songs instantly — recognized that unique bouncy-punk sound.

While Rafi was all Madonna and Lionel Richie and the Bangles, Penny was more the Smiths and the Cure and the Violent Femmes and the Hoodoo Gurus. And even a band called the The, which Rafi thought was about the wittiest name she'd ever heard for a band in her entire life.

She had her folder open on her lap and was checking through the steps of a maths problem when she heard it — a voice at the door of Penny's flat, a slight tapping against the door as her mum said, *"Rafaela. Abre. Soy yo."*

Rafaela. Open up. It's me.

Rafi's mum had been remarkably calm last night when she came home from work to find her paintings of La Llorona all bundled up by the front door. She looked around at the bare walls, the cleared surfaces and said quietly almost to herself — perhaps mostly to herself — "I did them to keep her away from us."

She squatted down by the still-open front door and undid the twine around one of the bundles of drawings, looking at the horse-headed woman she'd drawn over and over and over again.

"Am I crazy?" she said even more quietly.

Rafi squatted beside her, feeling a flutter of panic unpeeling inside.

"What? Of course not. No. It's just something you like to do."

Her mum took the Minty horse heads from the shoebox, then lined them up on the palm of her hand in rows like a battalion of horse-headed soldiers.

"People say she's not true," she said, touching the little figures. "But I know what I saw that day. And too many people have seen her over the years for her not to be true. Remember the children before Tonio? That baby in the flats next door to our place? Remember her?"

Rafi nodded.

"Coming here, I thought I'd got away from her. Then last year she showed up again. She found me. I've got rid of her now, though, and she's not coming back."

Rafi felt a shiver running the length of her body.

"No one understands what it's been like for me," her mum went on, slipping into Spanish. "Not you. Not your uncles. No one. He was three …" Her voice was barely a whisper now. "I never saw him write his own name or bring a friend home from school or any of those things a mother needs to see. I don't know if he's here with us, or if he's stuck in La

Paz wondering where we are. If he's in heaven or in limbo because he was taken at the wrong time. Sometimes I hardly remember him. I can barely see his face in my head these days. He's foggy."

Rafi understood that part. Tonio was like a wisp of smoke she couldn't hold onto. Vague. The merest whiff of a memory.

The worst thing, though, was that Rafi didn't really miss him. Not if she was being honest. Not like her mum did. She didn't think about him every day. She could go for months without even remembering that she used to have a little brother.

Rafi touched her mum's hand, feeling a shift in the way she felt about her. Her mum was heartbroken, that was all, and Rafi could never make up for it, no matter how hard she tried, because she wasn't the one who'd broken her mum's heart — Tonio was.

Rafi's mum looked at her, shaking her head a little as if realizing only then that she'd been speaking out loud. She clicked her tongue at Rafi and stood up, going into the kitchen.

"*Rafaela. Abre,*" her mum said now through the door to Penny's flat.

Rafi opened the door.

"Frenchie's on the phone," her mum said, her lips tight, disapproving of Frenchie calling this late — eight-thirty on a Saturday night, for goodness' sake.

"Oh," Rafi said. "Okay. Tell her I'll call her back from here."

Her mum nodded, crossing the hallway back to their flat and shutting the door without another word.

"Oh my God," Frenchie said, picking up the phone on the first ring, not even checking first that it was Rafi. "Rafi. You've got to cancel babysitting. There's this big party tonight, I've just heard about it."

Rafi flopped her head back. Typical.

"I can't," she said.

"You have to," Frenchie said, a disaster-zone tone entering her voice. "Diff's going to be there."

"Diff? But Penny's left already. I can't exactly leave Joshie here alone."

"Is he asleep?"

"Yeah."

"So, he'll be fine."

Rafi couldn't tell if Frenchie was serious or joking.

"Tell your mum you're going out for a while, and to go in to him if he wakes up. Tell her you'll leave the door open so she can hear."

"Sure," Rafi said. "As if."

"She's just at home, she's not doing anything. Ask her to babysit for you. Or take him into your place, and she can look after him there. Doesn't matter how it happens, but you can't miss out on this. Seriously. It's going to be huge. Everyone's going. I'm coming over now. I'm not taking no for an answer. We can tram it from yours. It's just over the river in South Yarra. Not far. Come on."

Rafi could just imagine her mum's response if she asked her.

Lo siento, Rafaela, she would say, tight-lipped. I'm sorry, Rafaela. *Pero no puedo.* But I can't.

"Oh God, come on," Frenchie said. "Go and tell your mum it's the biggest party ever. Tell her you'll do anything, wash the dishes for a month, but she has to babysit for you."

"I'm not sure Penny would be all that happy to come home and find out that I split."

Although actually, Rafi thought, of anyone, Penny would

be the most likely to understand the importance of her going to this party. Diff was going to be there.

Diff. Breathe in. Cameron. Breathe out.

"We can get back before her," Frenchie said. "You don't even have to tell her if you don't want to. I'll come home with you. But you've *got* to come. It's going to be *huge*."

Rafi considered it for a moment.

The worst her mum could say was no. But maybe she'd say yes. Maybe she'd remember being young herself once and wanting desperately to go to a party and see the handsome boy that she was maybe going to marry one day.

It was a long shot, but worth a try.

She told Frenchie she'd call her back.

Crossed the stairwell to her own flat. To her mum.

"Ma?" she said, opening the door with her key.

Her mum was sitting on the couch watching television.

"Ma," Rafi said, trying on a voice that maybe, maybe would work. "There's this party on tonight. The biggest party ever. Everyone's going to be there. And I know I'm supposed to be babysitting, but Joshie's fast asleep, he won't wake up, he never does no matter what, he's such a good sleeper, and I was thinking that maybe, if I could go for a couple of hours ..."

And then she stopped, because some things didn't need explaining. She wanted to go. She needed her mum to babysit for her. It was out of her hands.

Her mum looked up at Rafi, her lips pushing out with all the disapproving things that were inside her mouth. She looked at the telly.

And then she looked up at Rafi again, a smile relieving her face in a way that Rafi hadn't seen in a long time. Maybe forever.

111

"Well, I shouldn't ..." her mum said.

"I know. I know it's really bad and really irresponsible and I would never ask you except it's the one party I really want to go to, and you know how hard I study, and I'll do anything, anything, if you'll look after Joshie for me just for a couple of hours."

"What time will you be home?" her mum asked.

And Rafi did something that she never, ever did. She ran over and hugged her mum.

The Guy

No matter how firmly you held your foot over the drain in the shower, you could never stop the water from going down the plughole. Guy knew. He'd tried. He couldn't even get it up to ankle level. It was impossible.

A bit like tonight.

No matter how hard he tried, he couldn't stop people from coming inside. At one stage he stood at the front door telling them they couldn't, but it was like one of those dreams where you were trying to speak but no sound came out, because no matter what he said, no one seemed able to hear him. He kept shutting the door, and someone kept opening it to let more people in. There must have been two hundred or three hundred people in his house, and still more were turning up.

He was trying to stop the water from going down the drain, but the water kept burbling down anyway.

The music was blasting, there were bottles everywhere, the house was bulging, fit to go *ba-doing* from all the people in there, someone was vomiting in the garden, there were a bazillion cigarette butts in the grass, a guy and girl he didn't know were going upstairs to the bedrooms.

And the strange fact was, three hours ago there were four of them hanging out in the kitchen: him, Benj, Liv and Mish.

And then the doorbell rang. And three hundred people turned up at his house for a party.

Not all at once, of course. It had been more of your standard pyramid-type arrangement than your straight-into-it massive party.

First of all, Matty McD. and Rob and Bill and a few others turned up. The tip of the pyramid.

Then came Liz and Sally and Lindy and Sarah and Kate and Simonette and Simone and Alison and Margie and a bunch of Mandeville girls. The next level down.

Then Wilbur and Tim and Adam and Chris and Anna and Gin and Doone and Luke and Clare and about ten other people Guy didn't know but who were friends of friends arrived.

After that, the pyramid took on a life of its own. Tier after tier of people — random people that no one even knew — stacking up like a circus act, *ta-dah*, adding layer after layer. People started carrying the furniture out of the house so there was more room for people inside, and even without furniture it was still really squashed, and still more people kept barging in with their beers and their joints and their girlfriends and their boyfriends, and Guy stopped trying to bounce people out because it was like trying to stop water going down the drain. It wasn't going to happen.

People were squished into the hallway and up the stairs and in the lounge room and in the kitchen and in the TV room and in the front yard and out the back and on the nature strip, and they were spilling out onto the road, nearly being run over by the occasional car.

It was lucky Guy lived in a quiet street.

The night had warped into an altered dimension. The handbrake on the world had been released, and the party careened like a rogue elephant in a china shop. Or was that supposed to be a bull?

It reminded Guy of the Cat in the Hat stories, which would start off with just one small something — a pink spot on the mum's dress, say — and then get worse and worse. Pink bath rings and gloop dripping down the walls and pesky Thing One and Thing Two causing trouble — until it was seriously out of control. Guy had found those books really stressful when he was a kid. The way the Cat in the Hat would keep insisting everything was fine, relax, while he balanced the fish in the bowl on a rake and jumped on a ball and added a cake and books and flowers, and you knew it was going to end badly but there was nothing you could do about it.

Standing in his house on this particular Saturday night, Guy felt Cat-in-the-Hat-stressed, although he still had hopes that he'd be able to keep the party secret from his olds.

He assembled a plan in his brain. He and Benj and Mish and whoever else stayed the night would clean like crazy people tomorrow. They'd pick up all the beer bottles, glasses, cigarette butts, bottles of Great Western and general crap. They'd replace all of his parents' alcohol that had been drunk (the gin could be topped up with water, the Pimm's replaced with black tea), vacuum the house top to bottom, put the furniture back — job done.

But for now, everyone was in his house and there was nothing he could do about it. So, like the Cat in the Hat before him, he decided he'd bounce on the ball with the fish on the rake, and fix it all when the time came.

He went into the front room and started dancing around like a maniac with Benj and Ash, fists pumping the air, jumping up and down, having a good time.

And smashed some chick he'd never seen before right in her face with his elbow.

The Girl

As it turned out, Rafi and Frenchie didn't even need the address of the party. Knowing the name of the street was enough.

They got off the tram at the corner of Chapel Street and Toorak Road with a few other kids their age — people they didn't know — and turned left along with everyone else, down Toorak Road, past the shops, looking in the windows at the clothes they might buy when they were older and working in proper jobs.

"You going to this party?" one of the guys asked them as they walked through the park at the start of Rockley Road.

"Yeah," Frenchie said.

And then they heard it. Tendrils of music wafting down Rockley Road toward them. Their ears pricked at the music and they followed it, knowing that where there was loud music, there was a party happening.

And how right they were.

The closer they got, the louder the music, till they arrived out in front of Party Central, furniture jumbled in lounge-room formation, except instead of carpet there was lawn, and instead of walls there were trees and side fences.

Frenchie knocked Rafi with her elbow.

"Worth skipping babysitting for?"

Rafi grinned.

The chilled winter air was defrosted by all the laughter and flirting coming from hundreds of people. The lights from the house cast a warm yellow glow over all those cold faces.

Groups of guys were chugging down beers and glancing over at groups of girls, who were passing around plastic cups filled with cheap bubbles. One person's back would meet someone else's back and they'd turn around, laugh, introduce themselves and start talking, maybe kiss, maybe dance, whatever took their fancy.

Butterfly-girls were alighting first on one group then another, flirting, meeting guys, moving on, meeting more guys, the nectar of their flirty conversation sweetening the mood, the guys laughing loudly, puffing out their chests, ignoring the girls but at the same time totally aware of them.

As Rafi and Frenchie moved through the crowd toward the house, they saw the Carey sisters — Jacki leaning into some guy, her face tilted up to his, Susan laughing at what appeared to be the funniest joke she'd ever heard. Lou was playing thumb-wars with Barnesy. Jack McCarthy was there. Rafi had met him at a party a couple of weeks ago and thought he was quite cute until Diff called her to him.

Daniella Patchett was there with her stepsister, Athina, the two of them closer than real sisters. There was Natalie Reage, over on exchange from Paris, who Frenchie seemed vaguely jealous of (Natalie's authentic Frenchness pipping Frenchie's inherited Frenchness at the post); Sav and Alice from Genazzano, who Rafi had had some big nights with; Buffy Brown and Anna Green, known collectively as the Colored Girls because of their surnames; and Michael King, who everyone called Wayne because, well, put "Wayne" with "King" and it was a whole lot funnier than plain old Michael.

Bernard Simson was in the hallway talking footy as usual with Harry Enfield and Charlie Wilson. So were the Gilot twins, one of who (Rafi could never figure out which) had been expelled for sneaking a girl into his room during the Head of the River trip earlier in the year. Ella and Yaz Keneally, Genny Winton and Dominique Shriver from Year Eleven were in the kitchen, along with half of Melbourne.

And there, leaning against the fridge, was Diff Cameron.

Diff, breathe in.

Cameron, breathe out.

Rafi walked through the kitchen, slowing as she went past Diff, maybe because there were lots of people and it was hard to walk through them all, or maybe because she wanted to make sure he noticed her. He looked up, raised an eyebrow at her, tipped some beer down his throat, then turned back to the girl he was chatting to.

His ex-girlfriend.

Rafi felt a buckling inside of herself as she watched him lean in and kiss her against the kitchen bench.

Rafi was out of there. She shoved through the jam of people in the hallway, out into a group jumping around like a bunch of idiots in the lounge room.

Diff couldn't give a shit about her. All these months she'd been thinking about him, daydreaming about him, kissing him when the opportunity arose, writing his name in her folders at school, trying to figure out how to end up as his girlfriend, and he couldn't have cared less.

The worst thing was that she knew she had no right to say anything to him. He'd never asked for her phone number. He'd never made her feel special. He'd never done a single thing that could be pointed at as proof that they had something going on. His modus operandi had been to simply hook up with her at the end of the night if he was in the mood. And she'd been the willing accomplice to her own humiliation.

She was going to walk all the way home. On her own. In the dark. It would serve Diff right if something bad happened to her.

And just as she thought this, a guy brought his arms down to pump the air one more time (because a hundred times were never enough) and elbowed her straight in the face.

Elbow.

Meet Face.

Because when you'd had a shit night, an elbow to the face was exactly how you wanted to top it off.

And then — because an elbow to the face wasn't quite perfection enough — her nose started to bleed all over the place.

Rafi sat on the edge of Party House's bathtub, her face tilted up toward the ceiling. Elbow Guy held a towel over her nose, keeping the back of her head steady with his other hand.

He was cute, Rafi couldn't help but notice. Not super-super cute, not Diff Cameron cute, but cute. He had dark hair and olive skin and these eyes that were a messed-up gray-blue and, well, basically Elbow Guy could work an entire magic act around those eyes — wave a watch in front of a person's face and have them flapping their arms like a chicken or mooing like a cow without them even realizing they were doing it.

Someone came into the bathroom. Rafi slid her eyes over to see who it was. She was hoping it was Diff, but no, it was just some random guy wanting to use the toilet in the adjoining room.

Rafi wanted to be home.

Elbow Guy took the towel away from her face and ducked his head to get a good look straight up her nose, which was excellent, because straight up her nose was definitely her most flattering angle.

"Looks like it's stopped," he said, going over to the sink to wet the towel and then using it to wipe her nose clean.

Thanks a lot, nose, Rafi felt like saying. *Appreciate it.*

Toilet Guy came out from the toilet, grabbed his beer off the basin and left. Without washing his hands, Rafi noticed. The guy before hadn't washed his hands, either. She wondered if this was a guy thing, or if it was just those two — coincidentally the only two guys at the entire party who didn't bother washing their hands after going to the toilet — happening to come in one after the other while she was in the bathroom. And either way, why wouldn't they wash their hands? They'd just been holding their old fellas, for God's sake. If ever there was a time to wash your hands, it would be after you'd been holding your penis, Rafi would have thought.

Elbow Guy finished wiping her blood away with the towel.

"I hope it's not broken," he said. Rafi was still thinking penis, but she was pretty sure he was talking nose.

"Four," she replied, holding up four fingers at him.

"What?"

"That's the fourth time you've said that," she said, looking into his eyes.

Yep, those eyes were still there in his face where he'd left them. If she wasn't careful she'd be clucking like a chicken before she knew it and have only herself to blame.

"Well, I'm just hoping it's not broken," he said, grinning. "Five," he added, before Rafi had a chance to.

He had a sweet smile. It warmed his face, crinkling his eyes and ripening his cheeks, as if he was an apple on a tree. Ready for picking.

Unfortunately, Rafi wasn't in the mood. All she wanted was to go home. Although it *was* nice sitting in the bathroom next to him. There was even a chance that maybe she didn't care as much about Diff kissing his ex-girlfriend as she thought she did.

Rafi sneaked another quick look at Cute Elbow Guy. He was looking straight at her, studying her — trying to figure out if he'd done any permanent damage to her face, she guessed.

She pinched her nose tentatively with her fingers, testing to see if there was anything broken in there.

"It's fine. Seriously, don't worry. It happens a lot."

He laughed. "You get elbowed in the face a lot?"

She sounded like an idiot.

"Blood noses." She looked from his smile to his hands resting palms down on the edge of the bath. "Okay, I haven't had one for ages, but tonight, you know …"

Yes. He knew. He'd been there when it happened. He and his elbow had been there.

"You sure you're okay?" he said.

"I'm fine." Rafi risked another quick glance at his face.

Elbow Guy took a swig of his drink, then passed it to Rafi. For a moment she considered settling back into the slump she'd fallen into over Diff, but maybe a couple of drinks — a bit of Dutch Courage — was exactly what she needed. She'd go back downstairs and slap Diff across the face, very dramatic.

She'd say to him, "Don't ever ..."

What? Call her again? He didn't anyway. Kiss her again? Didn't look like that was likely. Talk to her again? There wasn't a whole lot of talking that had gone on between them in the first place. Theirs hadn't exactly been a meeting of the minds. A meeting of the mouths was about as good as it got.

Anyway, she didn't want to slap him, now that she thought about it. Slapping him would make him think she cared, and she didn't anymore. Sitting in the bathroom with blood all down the front of her dress, she didn't care anymore.

"You know," Rafi said, tipping the whatever-it-was down her throat, starting to like the fact that they were still sitting in the bathroom even though they could have gone back downstairs now that her nose wasn't gushing blood all over the place, "they should make a drink called Dutch Courage. UDL should. With schnapps, or whatever the national Dutch drink is. Everyone would buy it, because that's the point, isn't it — to get a little Dutch Courage. What do you think?"

"Genever," he said.

"What?"

The noise from the party downstairs was bouncing off the bathroom tiles. It sounded like he'd said "jenever," but that couldn't be right because there wasn't even such a word.

"It's kind of a cross between vodka and gin," he continued. "Genever. If it's called Dutch Courage, it would need to be made with genever."

Rafi looked at him for a moment.

"Right," she said skeptically. "So you just happen to know off the top of your head what the national drink of ... of the Dutch is?"

As she was saying it, she was trying to remember what the name of the country Dutch people lived in was. Amsterdam? Denmark?

"What can I say?" he said. "I know my stuff."

"Well ... genever heard of such a ridiculous thing in my entire life," Rafi said, and then laughed at her own joke.

It occurred to her that maybe she was a bit drunk. Or maybe the elbow to her nose had given her a bit of a concussion.

He grinned at her again.

"I'm Dutch," he said, and then thought a moment. "Well, Australian, but my mum's Dutch."

"Oh. Well, then, I guess you've got the whole Dutch Courage thing already, without needing any of this?" Rafi said, holding up the bottle.

"It's part of my DNA," he said.

Rafi frowned. "So if you're Dutch, where's your accent?"

"Don't need one. Brave enough without it."

The party had cranked up a notch by the time they got back downstairs.

People were dancing everywhere, and all available surfaces were filled with bottles. Cigarette butts polka-dotted the floor. A garden rake — bizarrely — was standing beside the doorway. And music had taken over the house. Every nook, every cranny, every corner, every wall, every person was music. There was no room for anything else. Nothing else could fit. It was impossible not to dance. It was audio perfection. It just didn't get any better.

Rafi started moving, the music soaking into her like she was a sponge, and Guy — that was his name, Elbow Guy — came so close to her that if she shut her eyes she could feel the heat of his body running the length of hers, against her thighs, close to her stomach, warming her torso.

He put his hands on her hips, and Rafi breathed in.

The music was deep down inside her chest now. Her body felt every note, every lyric. Guy moved in close, in sync with her hips. She looped her arms over his head and relaxed against his body, moving in as close to him as she could possibly get, his hands on her hips, gripping her not hard but firmly, bringing her against him, against him and the music.

He leaned down and his mouth brushed her mouth, and Diff was nothing. Diff never felt like this. This was something else altogether. Ex-girlfriend could have Diff, and good luck to her.

Guy's mouth opened slightly, just slightly, no pressure, no expectation, but expecting no rejection, either. Then his tongue was inside Rafi's mouth, his arms bringing her body in to him — closer, closer — the heat of the room not oppressive anymore, their own internal mercury soaring.

"You wanna go to my room?" he whispered straight into her mouth, the words bypassing her ears and going straight down to her stomach.

And as they kept kissing, she nodded.

Because right then, right there that minute, she really, really, really wanted to go to his room.

Badly.

Guy and Rafi lay length by length on his bed, his flesh and blood running up against hers.

Rafi unlatched her lips from his and moved her head away, trying to slow them both down, but he kept kissing her — her neck, her shoulder, her ear, and as he kissed her she leaned back into him because there was nothing in the world that had ever felt so good.

Rafi pulled her mouth away for a second time and took a deep breath, blowing out slowly and deliberately.

"I have to go in one minute," she said.

"Okay," he said.

And he started kissing her again. Resistance was useless. This guy, this mouth, these hands … Rafi was powerless to stop him. Or, okay, that wasn't true, but why would she want to? Why on earth would she want to stop feeling like this?

She pulled her mouth away from his again. If she didn't get some space, if she didn't get some air, she wasn't sure what would happen. Although she suspected that if she didn't get some space, whatever happened would be absolutely brilliant.

You only just met him, her brain said.

But it feels so good.

He might be using you, her brain said.

He's not using me. I can tell.

You've been drinking. You'll regret it.

So what if I'm drunk. Who cares?

You have to get back to Joshie.

"I've got to get back to Joshie," Rafi repeated out loud. "I'm supposed to be babysitting him. My mum's looking after him for me, but I said I'd be back before twelve."

Guy lay back from her and put his hands behind his head, grinning.

"The night is but a puppy," he said, his entire body open to her, an invitation for her to lean forward and continue where they'd left off.

"I can't," she said. "I have to go. And I've gotta find my friend."

Demonstrating a strength of character she didn't know she had, Rafi stood up from the bed and looked down at Guy. Keeping distance between them was the only thing that would help her stick to her plan of being home before twelve.

He stood up and brought her toward him one last time.

"I'll walk you out," he said.

They walked, fingers entwined, through the party, looking for Frenchie. She wasn't anywhere in the house, so they squeezed their way through the crowd out to the front yard.

Rafi looked around. She had to go, but she didn't want to leave Frenchie on her own.

Then she saw her, resting back against a tree in the front yard, a guy leaning over her, Frenchie looking up into his face. Rafi knew that stance. If she was Frenchie, she wouldn't want to be going anywhere. But she went over to check anyhow, dragging Guy through the hordes.

"I've got to go," Rafi said to her. "You coming?"

Frenchie raised her eyebrows at Rafi.

"You okay if I stay?" she asked.

"Sure."

Rafi gave Frenchie a hug, then turned back to Guy.

"She's going to stay. I might need a taxi. Can you call me one?"

Guy put his hand up to her head, his mouth in her hair.

"Where do you live?" he said into her ear.

"Richmond," Rafi said. "Just over the bridge. Not far. I could practically walk, except I don't have time."

And then he took her by the shoulders and looked her straight in the eye. As if what he was about to say was the most important thing she'd ever hear in her life. Ever.

"Wait here," he said. "Don't go away."

And then he turned around and went back inside.

The Guy

Even with a towel covering up most of her face, Guy could tell this girl was gorgeous.

He took the towel away and looked at her nose. It was sweet. A small, neat nose with freckles splashed across it. Unless that was blood. It could be blood.

He got up and wet the towel, then wiped her nose like she was a kid, checking. No, they were freckles. And now that he'd taken the towel away, he could have a proper look at the whole package.

He liked.

He kept asking if her nose was okay, checking that her nose wasn't broken, looking at her face from different angles, but to be honest, that was a ploy. A way of talking to her and looking at her — really looking at her, without seeming like he was checking her out.

He took a swig from his bottle, then handed it over for her to share.

The way she put her lips around the neck made him think bad things. Very bad things. Very bad as in very good things.

And then she started talking about Dutch Courage and made that pun about genever, and Guy wanted to pop her in his pocket and keep her. Pretty *and* funny.

He took her back downstairs and they started dancing.

He took her back upstairs.

Into his bedroom.

More dancing. A different kind.

This girl lying beneath him … he kept his weight on his arms because he didn't want to crush her. He didn't want to put his full weight on her, but on the other hand he wanted to engulf her. He wanted to be entirely over every inch of her body. He wanted the two of them to merge into one.

He rolled over onto his back so that she lay along the length of him. That way he didn't have to worry about crushing her.

This girl … well, shit, Sherlock, he hadn't felt like this about a girl for, maybe, ever.

And then she rolled off him and said she had to go.

As they walked out of the house and into the front garden, through the throngs of people and upended furniture, he saw the one thing that had the potential to get him into a whole lot of trouble. Real trouble. *Serious* trouble.

His mum's new car was in the carport and people were sitting on the bonnet, leaning against it, maybe scratching it.

This was very bad news. If anything happened to that car, his mum would kill him. Party: problem. Car: major problem.

Rafi spotted her friend who was getting cozy with one of the guys from the footy club. Her friend checked Guy out, then looked back at Rafi and said something, but Guy wasn't listening.

He needed to get those people off his mum's car. If he moved it out of the garage, parked it on the street a few doors up from his house, that might work.

"She's going to stay," Rafi said to him. "I might need a taxi. Can you call me one?"

And then Guy had the perfect idea. It would give him more time with Rafi. And it would sort out the car problem.

"Where do you live?" he asked, bringing her in close to him because really, he couldn't get enough of her.

"Richmond. Just over the bridge. Not far. I could practically walk, except I don't have time."

"Wait here. Don't go away."

He ran back inside, pushed his way through the crush of people into the kitchen, grabbed his mum's car keys off the hook in the pantry.

Then he went back outside.

Rafi was standing under the tree he'd left her by, looking around, seeming uncertain as to whether she should keep waiting or go.

He waved to her and ran over, chucking his mum's car keys in the air and hacky-sack-nudging them with his shoulder back to his hands.

"I'll drive you," he said.

"Oh. You've got your license?"

"I've gotta move my mum's car anyway, so it's just as easy to drive you home," he replied.

Which, of course, wasn't answering the question. Not even a bit.

The Girl

The post-kissing conversation — in Rafi's limited experience, at least — was always the most difficult.

The pre-kissing conversation was flirty and easy, mainly because Rafi usually didn't know it was a pre-kissing conversation until after the kissing had started, so she didn't have any pre-kissing nerves.

The mid-kissing conversation was fun because if you couldn't think of anything to say, you simply put your mouth back on theirs and continued the pash-fest to cover up any awkward silences.

But the post-kissing conversation was always uncomfortable. She'd try to think of something to say, and the harder she thought, the less anything to say would pop into her head. That was how it had always been with Diff, especially. Stilted, awkward, post-kissing non-conversation.

But with Guy, it wasn't like that at all.

He asked her why she had to babysit so late — "Long story" — and why he'd never seen her before — "I've been hiding" — and what she was doing tomorrow. Maybe she'd like to come round to his place and help them clean up.

"Especially," he said, "seeing as you're the one who made all the mess."

Rafi laughed.

She asked him all about the party — "It was only supposed to be a few friends" — and where his parents were — "Skiing for the weekend" — and what they were going to say about the party when they got home tomorrow night — "Nothing, because they won't know it happened."

The only thing they didn't talk about was whether he had his driver's license. She was pretty sure he didn't, but if she was to be completely honest, she was more than happy having him drive her.

She needed to get home before Penny. He was driving her. That was as much information as she needed. Finding out that he didn't have his license would only complicate things.

"It's just here," Rafi said as he turned into her street, pointing to her block of flats with the darkened bistro below.

Guy slowed the car and pulled over to the curb, leaned over and kissed her.

"I'm glad I elbowed you in the nose," he said softly.

"Bastard," she said, smiling through the kiss.

"You don't really have to come and help clean up tomorrow — you weren't really the messiest one there — but I'd like to see you again," he said into her hair. "Can I have your number?"

"Sure."

Definitely.

She wrote it down for him on an old tram ticket she found in her bag.

"I'll call," he said, holding the tram stub like it was a golden lottery ticket.

"I'll answer," she said back.

She ran down the side path to the stairwell.

Sweet guy. Sweet, handsome, not-bastard Guy.

She ran up the stairs taking them two at a time, imagining what would have happened if she hadn't gone to the party.

It would, she thought, have been a disaster. An absolute disaster. There would have been every chance she would never have met Guy. She was so glad Frenchie had persuaded her to go.

She was so glad her mum had babysat.

She knocked on the door to Penny's flat and waited for her mum to open up.

She jiggled where she was standing, muttering to herself, "Come on, come on, open up. Open the door."

Now that she was here waiting to be let back into Penny's flat, she realized how much she didn't want Penny to arrive home and see her standing in the stairwell waiting to be let in.

Not that it would really matter. Penny would be fine with it, because it wasn't that big a deal. She'd only gone out for a couple of hours, and by the way how about this new guy she'd met, Guy, so cute, and also what about Diff Cameron, what a bastard, just like Penny's Bastard Ex.

But still, Rafi decided that she would prefer it if Penny didn't come home right at that moment.

Not because there was any problem with it, but Penny might — well, she'd be fine, but maybe she wouldn't think it was completely brilliant that Rafi had gone out when she was supposed to be looking after Joshie.

Rafi was about to knock on the door again — her hand was raised — when she had a chilling thought.

Maybe Penny was already home in bed asleep. Maybe she'd left the band early and come home to find Rafi's mum babysitting Joshie.

Rafi's hand dropped down to her side.

Maybe the reason her mum wasn't answering the door was because she was home already.

Rafi turned around and looked at the door to her flat. Got out her keys and opened the door.

But the lounge room was empty. Silence.

She walked down the hallway to her mum's room. Not there.

Good.

Very good.

Excellent.

Rafi ran back out and knocked on the door of Penny's flat, waited only the shortest of short moments, then went to the pot plant and grabbed Penny's key from the soil.

Her mum was still there babysitting Joshie, probably asleep on the couch, and Penny was still out having a good time. Rafi would have to wake her mum up and get her out of there quick smart so Penny didn't walk in on the two of them.

She opened the door to Penny's flat and looked around.

It was silent inside. Vacant. Her mum wasn't in the lounge room and, strangely, the copy of *The Weeping Woman* that Penny's ex had done for her as a joke present had been moved from the mantelpiece to the couch.

Rafi walked down the hallway and looked in Joshie's room. His cot was empty. She went to the kitchen. Maybe he'd woken up, which he normally never did, and Rafi's mum was giving him another bottle.

No one was in the kitchen.

The flat was empty.

Rafi went back to the lounge room, looking around one last time. She couldn't get the situation straight in her head.

Joshie wasn't here. Her mum wasn't here. But where were they? Where had her mum and Joshie gone? There were only two places they could be. Penny's flat or Rafi's flat, and they were in neither.

She went back out to the stairwell and opened the door to her own flat again. No. No one was there. She stood between both flats, both doors open, uncertain what to do, where to stand, even.

And then she heard voices coming up the stairs. Soft voices, whispering, keeping quiet, not-wanting-to-disturb-anyone voices.

Just at exactly the wrong time.

Penny and Mick.

The Guy

It had been one of those seems-like-a-good-idea-at-the-time situations, and now Guy was stuck with it, driving his mum's car.

Unlicensed.

Drunk.

With Rafi in the car.

He couldn't help thinking about Rachel Henry.

Last year, Rachel Henry had been driving up to Mount Buller with Stu Milford. They'd had a couple of drinks, it was late at night, and Stu had driven off the mountain. He'd been fine. She'd been killed.

And here was Guy doing the same thing. The only difference was that he was unlicensed, whereas Stu had been on his Ps at the time.

He couldn't imagine what it would be like if he killed Rafi. Met her, fell for her, had a crash, killed her.

The problem was, he couldn't say he'd changed his mind — that maybe he shouldn't drive, maybe she should catch a taxi after all — because what sort of a dick offered to drive someone home and then remembered, when they were behind the wheel, that it wasn't such a great idea? That they didn't actually have a driver's license?

He turned right into Toorak Road (busy, bright, restaurants and cafés and traffic and people and potential police cars everywhere), then turned into the first side street (side streets being the preferred option of unlicensed drunk drivers), left onto Alexandra Avenue, right again over the bridge at Church Street and the rest of the way to Rafi's place.

He got her there. Made it. Got her home okay.

He delivered her to her building, watched her walk to her flat, looked at her phone number scratched onto the back of a tram ticket and smiled to himself.

It occurred to him that maybe he should leave the car at Rafi's place, come and pick it up the next day. It would be a good excuse to see her again. But driving home in broad daylight on a Sunday? Unlicensed? Nope. Definitely not a good idea.

He drove back down Church Street, back toward the party, driving as slowly as he possibly could without risking getting pulled over for driving too slowly.

Rafi.

She had this beautiful mouth.

Gorgeous hair.

Soft skin.

And she was funny and smart and easy to talk to.

Girls didn't get much better than that.

He drove slowly toward the bridge, hoping he didn't run into any cops on the way home. Or any traffic. Or any of his parents' friends.

Imagine that, he thought. If he stopped at the traffic lights and Liz and Andy pulled up next to him.

Oh look, Liz would say to Andy. *There's Pam's new car. I thought they'd gone skiing with Geoff and Amanda, but they mustn't have gone, because otherwise who's driving — Oh, it's, why …*

He needed to get home.

He'd park his mum's car a few houses up from his joint, maybe out the front of the Fethers' place. Or the Varrentis'. Or even on the other side, by the O'Hallorans' or the Winships'. Whatever. Then tomorrow he'd put her car back in the carport, clean the house, and hopefully not get caught out for having a party.

Or driving her car.

It was ridiculous that he had to wait until he was eighteen to get his license. He'd been tall enough, his legs had been long enough to push the pedals, for years. He'd driven the ute up at his uncle's farm. Same same, really, except without the traffic.

When he was in America for a couple of weeks at the end of Year Ten staying with friends of his parents, his buddy Charlie drove everywhere. The same age as Guy, he'd been sixteen and driving a car, which made perfect sense.

If Guy lived in America, he'd have his license.

If you thought about it, the only reason he wasn't allowed to drive was for geographical reasons. For southern-versus-northern-hemisphere reasons.

The lights turned green, and it was as he turned left off the bridge into Alexandra Avenue that he saw something.

Something that distracted him, made him mount the curb, sideswiping a street sign.

Sideswiping his mum's brand new car.

It was what he saw walking along the river that did it.

139

Guy sat in the car without moving for just a moment. Then he got out very slowly and carefully and looked at the front of the car.

It seemed okay. A bit of a scratch, but nothing too bad. Nothing his mum would notice unless she was looking for it.

He looked back down at what had distracted him by the river.

It was a person, but with a horse's head. A completely normal body but a horse's head. Pushing a pram.

Guy felt like he'd slipped into some kind of Twilight Zone version of *Mary Poppins*.

Mary Poppins as half horse.

It was creepy, whatever it was he was looking at. Even the way the horse-headed person was walking was creepy — all uncertain and awkward, as if they were hobbled, pushing the pram dangerously close to the edge of the river.

Dangerously close. They should move the pram away from the edge. He'd have moved the pram away, if it had been him.

And then, in that instant, they pushed the pram straight off the path and into the water, the handles-and-wheels part of it separating from the cot-bed part as the pram sailed through the air.

The horse person continued walking along the track in the direction they'd been heading, away from Guy, away from the pram, without even stopping to check that the pram was okay.

There mustn't have been a baby in there.

It was like that film he'd seen at Cinema 180 a couple of years back, standing inside the curve of the screen and swaying with everyone else as he watched. There'd been a motorbike racing through the streets of Paris, and then a woman with a pram stepped out in the path of the motorbike and you thought the baby was going to be killed, but the bike swerved, and as it swerved you realized the woman pushing the pram was actually an old bag lady and she had leaflets in the pram. It wasn't a baby at all.

That must have been the deal with this pram.

But as the cot part of the pram drifted down the Yarra in Guy's direction, he could see not leaflets, not brochures, but blankets — soft-looking blue blankets, and something kicking the blankets, chubby legs pushing the blankets up.

It was a baby. A real, live, not-brochures baby.

Guy ran down to the river's edge, wanting to call out to someone for help, but no one was there, and what would they do anyway? The pram was slowly sinking, and the baby was going to be gone in a minute. Sunk. Drowned.

He knew he had to dive in, but no one swam in the Yarra because it was a filthy, muddy mess, and besides, it would be winter-freezing cold. Also, there was quite a drop to get into the river, a good few feet, probably six feet or something. He'd have to dive in, and he might have been a good runner, but swimming wasn't his thing.

The pram was drifting farther and farther toward the center of the flow, and Guy thought he was probably already too late. He should have jumped in as soon as he saw the pram go in, but he didn't because he thought it was brochures, and now he was too late and the pram was going to sink.

But it was a baby in there, and before he thought too much more about it — the fact that he was in winter clothes, the fact that he had shoes on, and how was he going to get to the pram in time, and the water would be freezing, and what was the point because he probably wouldn't make it in time — he pulled his shoes off and jumped in.

141

The water was ice-cubes cold — couldn't-get-your-breath freezing. His top clung heavy on his frame, and the pram was a lot farther away than he'd thought it was.

He started kicking toward the pram, but he was slow, too slow, the drag of his clothes making him feel like he was swimming in syrup.

And all the time the pram was getting farther away from him.

He could see it was starting to dip in the water, the essentially boat-like structure of it getting waterlogged, and that at any moment it was going to glug up with water and sink to the muddy bottom.

He could feel his chest getting wheezy, the freezingness of the water making breathing hard. He could see the pram starting to sink lower, the water dragging on it, like a drowning person clutching for the closest thing.

He wasn't going to get there in time.

He kicked harder, more strongly, trying to reach the baby before the pram went down.

He got closer. The pram was tilting now, one end of it burbling as water found a way in, swallowing the pram even as Guy came within reach.

He could hear the baby wailing as the freezing water hit the tiny body, a plaintive cry rising up, calling out.

With a glugging sound, the water dragged the pram under the surface, and Guy realized he truly was too late.

He dived under the water, and the pram wasn't even there anymore, but he grabbed onto something.

Something that had risen like a bubble out of the pram as it sank.

He dragged it up to the surface and looked at it, at what he was holding in his hands.

A baby. A chubby little fresh-faced, blue-lipped, gasping-for-breath baby.

Guy would have thought that'd be it.

Baby rescued, deed done.

But no, that wasn't how things were panning out, especially with the banks of the river six feet above him and no way of getting out of the water, and a baby in his arms, which he was hugging close in an effort to keep it warm.

There were some facts about the Yarra River that Guy had never appreciated before, since he'd never been in it. Which was not surprising, because no one swam in it unless it was by accident. Freak accident.

The Yarra was deep as well as ball-tighteningly cold. And the edges of the river, the six-foot-high concrete walls that ran the length of it through the city, were coated in moss down at water level, making it impossible to get any kind of climbing-type purchase at all.

Guy's clothes were dragging him down, and the baby wasn't helping much, either. It kept grabbing at his face and clinging to his ears and breathing shallow and fast, shivering like it was trying to shake its very skin loose from its bones.

They'd been in the water for a while now, and Guy's movements were starting to become slow and labored. He felt sluggish, and he couldn't think too much about the dark water he was in, because if he thought about how dark the water was, he'd wonder what was swimming down there beneath him, and that line of thinking wasn't going to go anywhere good.

The more he tried not to think about it, the more he couldn't think about anything else. What was in there with him? He could feel things touching his ice-block feet.

He stayed close to the edge of the river trying to grab onto something, anything, but the water kept dragging him along, and the walls were mossy and high and slippery and impossible to grab hold of.

His feet were frozen solid by now. He was shivering — holding the baby as well as he could, but nearly shaking it out of his grasp with his own shivering.

His back felt defenseless. He kept feeling as though something could grab him, could be following him, and he wouldn't know until the last second.

He couldn't stop yawning. He could barely keep his eyes propped open. He kept wanting to put the baby down, but there was nowhere to put it, and he kept worrying that he might drop it by accident, let it fall out of his arms and drift down to the bottom of the dark river and never be seen again.

He had to keep hold of the baby. It was the only thing he could do.

And then he saw them. The boat sheds. The Melbourne Grammar and Melbourne Uni boat sheds. There was a jetty for the boats to launch from, so Guy started swimming one-armed — baby in the other — toward it. He could see a few people leaving the sheds, walking near the river, finishing up from some party or other.

He put the baby on the timber decking, the sliminess of the wood and the slickness of the baby working against him exactly at the moment when he needed things to go right.

He felt like he could hardly lift the baby, much less grab it if it fell back into the river. He wasn't even sure if the baby was still alive. It was floppy. Not moving.

He kept one hand on the baby, stopping its body from slipping back into the water, but he needed both hands to drag himself up, and he started thinking that maybe it didn't matter about him, because he was feeling so tired and the baby was dead and he couldn't get up onto the jetty, and if he let go of the baby, the baby would slide back into the river and he could climb out, but he didn't want to let go of the baby because it seemed wrong, even now, to let the baby fall back into the water.

He called out, but no one heard him.

He thought maybe he'd burrow in under the jetty. It would be warmer in under the timber, out from the freezing-cold night air. But he couldn't burrow, because he needed to hold onto the baby. The poor baby.

The poor baby who lay on the slimy timber deck with its blue lips and its limp arms.

The poor baby.

Not the Party

The Ex

The Crystal Ballroom was all sticky carpet and cigarette smoke and body-slamming music. The Withers had come and gone, and John Lydon (ex-Johnny Rotten) had just taken the stage. He gripped the microphone in his fist and yelled, "God Save the Queen," out to the audience, riling them up and making Penny feel chalky and brittle. She hadn't realized punk was still such a big thing in Melbourne. She thought it had died back in the late seventies, but apparently not. Not if the spiky, safety-pinned crowd at the Crystal Ballroom was anything to go by.

Mick leaned into Penny's thoughts.

"Another drink?" he yelled.

She smiled at him. He looked handsome in his black T-shirt and faded jeans, and he'd been really sweet to her all night. Sweet and friendly and, well, just like a mate.

She was starting to think that her self-doubting with Rafi earlier had been correct, and this was just mates seeing a band after all.

"They're friends of mine," he'd said to her the other day about the Withers, the band who'd opened tonight. "They're

149

really good, and they're playing at the Crystal Ballroom this weekend, supporting John Lydon. You know? From the Sex Pistols? Anyway, I'm going with some friends and I thought you might like to come."

Penny had never been a huge fan of the Sex Pistols when they were around, but she thought seeing John Lydon would be interesting, if nothing else. She remembered the rumors about the Sex Pistols from back in the seventies. That Johnny Rotten had green teeth because he never brushed them. That none of them could play instruments before they joined the band. That Sid Vicious was a serious psycho maniac (and that was before he killed his girlfriend Nancy).

They'd only been a band for such a short time, a few years, but they'd made such a huge impact with their anarchy and their lippyness, that she wanted to see what John Lydon was like without the backup of the Sex Pistols to make him interesting.

And, okay, to hang out with Mick.

Mick was handsome and kind of delicious. There was something raw about him, red-blooded. His cheeks were constantly flushed, healthy and hearty like a stew. His eyelashes were long and dark like a cow's; his arms were strong and muscular. And, like the farm boys back home, he always looked at her with a slight shyness, but also with an openness and quickness to make a joke that she found appealing.

He was funny and sweet and handsome ... the polar opposite of Luke.

Luke.

Unfortunately, if Luke wanted to get back with her she'd be an instant yes. She was on a maybe-date with Mick, but she'd piff him for Luke in a heartbeat. In a broken-heartbeat.

Although she liked Mick. She really did.

It's just that she liked Luke more.

She wondered what it must have been about her first date with Luke that made it so special … until she recalled that they'd never really done the first-date thing. She met him that night at Naughtons. They went back to his studio, and she never went home again. That was it.

Maybe that was the problem. Luke never had to make an effort with her. Never had to ask her on a first date. Rolling over in bed and asking her if she wanted something to eat was as much first dateness as they'd ever gotten around to.

"You want another drink?" Mick repeated, in case Penny hadn't heard him the first time. Which she hadn't. Her ears were full of John Lydon yelling into the microphone, but she knew what he'd asked her because she'd read his lips.

She looked at the empty glass she was holding in her hand, then glanced at her watch.

It was only twelve. Hardly what you'd call late.

But as she stood among the Mohawks and safety pins and chains and general don't-fuck-with-me crowd, she realized that until tonight, she hadn't been more than a few meters away from Joshie since he was born. Well, even before that. Since she'd got pregnant, if she was going to get all technical about it. It was like she was now permanently leashed to him, the reins lashed around her shoulders, and when he wasn't close by she noticed the straining of the ties that bound them.

She wanted to check on him.

Make sure he was sleeping safely.

She wanted to go into his bedroom and lean over his cot, smell him, put her hand on his chest, feel his breathing, so shallow his chest barely moved with each inhale and exhale.

She wanted to make herself a cup of tea.

A punk channeling his inner Sid slammed into her, then ricocheted back to his girlfriend, who was channeling her matching inner Nancy.

To say that the natives were getting restless was an understatement. More like the natives were getting ready to throw a few punches and fuck with whoever got in their way. Why? Because they could. Because they were punks. Because they liked being scary.

There'd already been a punch-up a few feet from where they were standing earlier, and Penny doubted that things were going to mellow anytime soon now that John Lydon held center stage. Instead, the schizo vibe in the room was cranking up and the mob was getting pushier, angrier by the minute.

The reins tightened around her chest.

On the one hand, it was a good feeling, being out and seeing a cool band. This wasn't a mum-type thing to do. It was a normal twenty-three-year-old-girl thing to do, and it felt liberating.

On the other hand, she was ready to go home.

She smiled at Mick again.

"Actually, I was thinking I might go," she yelled into his ear, trying to be heard over the music. "It's getting kind of late."

It wasn't.

"I'll drive you," Mick yelled back.

"What?"

"I'm happy to drive you."

"You don't have to." Penny put her hand on his arm for a moment, then took it off again. Suddenly shy. "I mean, your friends are here and I feel bad making you leave."

If this conversation went on any longer she was going to lose her voice — so few words, but screamed so loudly.

"It's fine," Mick yelled, his elbow knocked at that moment by someone dancing into him. Maybe deliberately, maybe not. "I'm happy to."

"You sure?"

"Definitely."

They drove down Punt Road, away from the punks, back toward her place, back to Joshie. The leash eased as the distance between Penny and Joshie lessened.

"They've been getting quite a few gigs," Mick said, talking about the Withers, "and now they're thinking about going over to Berlin because, well, do you know the band the Birthday Party? Nick Cave?" Penny nodded. "Those guys are in Berlin and going gangbusters, and my mates are talking about joining them. Apparently it's really hardcore over there and they love Aussie bands, so yeah, tonight might be one of the last times they play here for a while, so it's nice that you could come along."

He smiled at Penny.

"So what did you think?" he asked her.

"They were great," she said. "I loved them. I especially loved that song 'Drowning.' And the cover they did of 'Husk' was amazing."

And on they drove, up Punt Road, talking about bands and other stuff, whatever, an easiness settling over the two of them.

He turned off Punt into Cremorne, then left into Cherry Tree Lane and down to the cherry tree growing out of the bitumen, cracking up the road.

The bistro was quiet. Locked up. Dark.

Mick stopped the car. Turned off the ignition.

"Okay. Well," Penny said, feeling her breath catch suddenly at the closeness of him. "Thanks for asking me along. It was great. They were really good. Typical that I discover my new favorite band just as they're about to move to Berlin."

Mick laughed, his easy smile so handsome.

"You look beautiful tonight," he said. "I mean, you always look beautiful, but tonight you look extra."

He had a radio voice. Deep. Lionesque in its rumble.

Penny remembered reading once that when a lion roared, the vibrations traveled through the ground. Even if you were up to a kilometer away, you would feel the roar trembling against the soles of your feet, traveling up your legs.

That was how Mick's voice was. A low rumble that traveled from his chest and plugged straight into hers.

Did friends seeing bands tell each other that they looked beautiful?

"I should go," Penny said. "Babysitter," she added.

And on an impulse, an out-of-the-blue impulse coming directly from that normal twenty-three-year-old girl still buried somewhere within Penny, she leaned forward and gave him a kiss goodbye. It was just a quick push of her lips against his ... but it was a kiss nonetheless. Then she moved her head back away from him.

He was watching her. His eyes were on her face, and he was smiling, as if he knew exactly what was going to happen next. He leaned forward and pushed his lips back against hers, longer than the kiss she'd given him, longer than a friend's kiss to another friend. And then he opened his mouth, and she fell ...

Because kissing in the front seat of Mick's car was a little slice of heaven. And since she was out in front of the flat, since she could see it hadn't burned down, that everything was okay — the leash between her and Joshie was barely noticeable. Loose. Slack, even.

Penny felt emboldened. Liberated. Twenty-three years old and single.

"You want to come up?" she asked, breaking away for a moment.

She didn't want to stop kissing him, but she was conscious that the longer she kissed him in the car, the more she was going to have to pay Fifi for the privilege.

"Sounds good," he said, smiling at her.

They walked down the side path to the back. Started walking quietly up the stairs.

Penny put her finger up to her mouth to show him that they were in a strictly whispering-only zone. The last thing she needed was for Rafi's mum to come out and start hissing at her to shush.

It had happened before.

At the top of the stairs, Penny got a fright to see Fifi on the landing, the doors to both flats wide open.

"Fifi," Penny said. "What are you doing? You just gave me a heart attack. You know Mick?" she said, holding her hand toward Mick like she was a *Sale of the Century* model and Mick was the latest offer from the gift shop.

Fifi looked different. She wasn't wearing the clothes she'd had on when Penny had left. She had her hair tied in two long plaits. She looked like she was ready to go partying or something. Although she wasn't smiling. In fact, she looked pale and very unwell.

Fifi gasped, breathless, "Penny ... I ... I ..."

And in that moment, Penny knew that something truly terrible had happened to Joshie.

The Artist

R eal didn't get back from Adelaide until very late. It was close to midnight by the time he answered his phone to Luke.

"We've got a problem," Luke said into the pub's payphone. "It's all over the papers. Some rumor about a buyer in Adelaide, and Dipper wants to know what's going on."

He looked over at Dipper, who was watching Luke closely from his position at the bar, a cigarette unsmoked in his hand.

"It's late," Real complained. "I've been driving for ten hours."

"Real, he says the cops are onto him. He's genuinely about to crack. We always said if it got to this point, you had a plan, a way to deal with it."

Luke could hear Real click his tongue down the phone.

There was silence.

And then finally he said, "I'll see you at the gallery in fifteen minutes."

The phone went dead in Luke's hand.

A few months ago, after the tequila lunch, Real called Luke and asked if he wanted to come in to discuss having an exhibition at Real's gallery.

They sat in the office at the back of the gallery on Chapel Street, Real on the business side of his desk nursing a Scotch on the rocks, Luke on the client side gripping a stubby of VB, just the two of them.

The conversation had wandered once again onto the idea of stealing the Picasso — how they could do it, when, ransom demands, that type of thing — when Real skewed the conversation in a direction that Luke hadn't been expecting.

"When I was younger," Real said, leaning back in his chair and taking a deep slug of his Scotch, "I always thought I'd be a painter. Like you. I could draw anything. Had a freakish memory for things I might have seen once. Art was the only thing I worked hard at. Everything else was a bore to me. Mundane. Others could do the maths, the Spanish, the history. Me, I was the artist. I was certain that was where I was headed."

He looked at Luke, watched him closely as he folded his arms across his chest and puffed on his stumpy cigar.

"Every spare moment," he went on, "I was painting. Drawing. In maths, the number four would always have a face in it. The number eight was always a woman with big hair. When I had to hand in an essay, I would spend more time working on the first letter of the first word — drawing an ornate scene around the capital letter like those monks from the Middle Ages used to — than I would on the rest of the essay in total."

He puffed more thick, pungent smoke in Luke's direction.

"I moved to Paris when I was fifteen," he said. "Couldn't get away from Colombia quick enough. But nothing happened.

158

My big career didn't appear. No one bought my work. I became one of those clichés, living in Paris, arguing with friends in cafés, drinking till all hours, calling myself an artist but not actually selling anything. At one stage someone asked me to paint a portrait of their dog. Their dog! Can you imagine?"

He leaned forward and tapped the end of his cigar against the crystal ashtray. The ash broke off in a thick chunk.

"One day, a friend came around — one of those wealthy housewife types who thinks hanging out with artists makes her a bohemian. In the hallway of my apartment was a rough sketch I'd done. Something I liked very much. It had a good line to it, similar to the type of thing my friend Giacometti did. It was something I was trying out. *He's popular*, I'd thought to myself. *Maybe if I do something more like him, people will buy me.*

"My friend, she looked at my sketch and she said, *Oh, Real, when did you get this? It's darling.* She asked if I'd sell it. I knew she'd mistaken it for Alberto's. She thought she was getting an original Giacometti at a bargain-basement price."

He patted his hair down, a frequent gesture of his.

"So I sold it to her." He took another puff of his cigar. "And why wouldn't I? I needed the money. I didn't lie, exactly. I just didn't tell her it was one of mine. And anyway, she was perfectly happy to rip me off. I thought that would be the last I'd hear of it. She was happy. I was happy. But she came back, sniffing around for something else she could buy. So I sold her another one." He pushed his mouth into a sly smile as he thought of the deal he'd made. "Another little sketch I'd whipped up. She became one of my best customers."

He stubbed his cigar out half finished and rested it on the edge of his ashtray.

"As it turned out," Real said, getting to the point of it all, "I was better at churning out Giacometti's work than I was at churning out my own. And it wasn't just Giacometti. It was Dubuffet, Vasarely, Locardi. All these friends of mine, I could mimic their lines, copy their composition. It turned out I was an excellent forger.

"One day" — he took a sip from his glass — "I decided to try something a little different. A little more ambitious. I had some old linen I'd bought from a furniture upholsterer I knew who'd gone out of business. I stretched it onto a frame and painted up a scene straight out of Monet. Just to see if I could."

He looked into the glass at the Scotch, the level of which was getting lower and lower.

"I took it to a dealer on the outskirts of Paris. Someone I didn't know and wasn't likely to run into. I explained that my father had been a diplomat and had owned quite a bit of artwork when I was growing up. I told him my sister had sent this piece to me to see how much I could sell it for.

"So. This gallery owner, he was interested, but he wasn't sure about provenance. How could he know it was a genuine Monet, he asked. Where was the paperwork? I told him that all I had was a very old receipt from when Father bought it all those years ago — I'd picked up an old receipt book at a flea market — and that I wanted to know how much it was worth now.

"This dealer, he took my painting away. Said he'd get back to me. I still remember the feeling, the anxiety, sure I'd get caught as I waited for him to decide whether it was genuine or not. I went back a few days later. The fellow told me he'd made some inquiries, and he could get a good price for it. And so, my career as an artist, as a forger, took off."

Luke watched Real, curious to see where exactly this confession was leading.

"Sometimes I nearly got caught, thanks to a composition that wasn't quite right, colors that were deemed inauthentic, a hand that didn't have the same lightness … But over time, as I developed my hand, I realized that there were certain painters I could mimic with ease. I was good with Matisse, for example. I made a lot of money selling him to Americans. At the beginning I used an easy, flowing line, because I thought Matisse had a very simple line, but once I realized his hand was not as secure as mine — that when he stopped work to glance up at his model, his line stopped, too, with just that tiny little bit of uncertainty — I learned to hesitate also.

"I always thought Matisse was a mediocre painter, greatly overrated. He juggled with colors and lines very cleverly, but to be clever is one thing and to be a great artist is something else. He was far and away the easiest artist to fake."

"So the things I've heard are true, then," Luke said, slugging back his beer.

"Oh, not all of them, darling, surely not," Real said with a sly chuckle. "I'd have been a very busy boy if *all* the rumors you've heard were true. But yes, some of them, sometimes, they are true."

"You were in jail in Marrakesh?"

"Untrue."

"Some big Texas businessman wants your scalp?"

"True." And Real laughed heartily. "But he was a buffoon. He deserved it."

He looked at Luke, his face showing that he knew he hadn't made his purpose quite clear yet.

"The point is, my dear" — and he leaned toward Luke as if he was going to whisper something just for the two of them, even though it was only the two of them in the room — "I can show you how it's done. You need to be very good — better than good — to fool the experts. And that's what we'd be up against if we painted a copy of *The Weeping Woman*."

Luke frowned. "What? Why would I paint a copy of *The Weeping Woman*? I thought we were talking about stealing it, not forging it."

"Because." Real leaned back, smoothed out a crease in his shirt. "My dear, that's where things get really fun. I've thought for a long time that you have a similar line to Picasso. A similar sensibility. With your talent and my connections, we could make a lot of money. I've got a buyer already. Someone who's very interested. I'm talking hundreds of thousands of dollars. We steal the painting, sell it to my buyer, return your forgery to the gallery ... everyone's happy."

Luke wasn't sure what to say. He had to hand it to Real. He was one cool cucumber. Somehow the conversation they'd had about stealing *The Weeping Woman* — which, it had to be said, had been strange in and of itself — had just taken an even stranger turn.

"For you to paint *The Weeping Woman* — a convincing copy — would be something you could do like this." And Real clicked his fingers to illustrate how easy it would be.

Luke didn't say anything.

The person Luke most admired, the artist he most copied, was Picasso.

Come on, he thought, everyone copied someone. There was no true originality in the world. The trick was to copy the people you admired most, but always with enough of a difference to get away with it.

The animals in Luke's paintings? Picasso's Minotaur.

The tribal patterns? Picasso's modernism.

"Dipper would never go for it," Luke said finally.

Real frowned.

"You mention Dipper because …?"

"Dipper has to be in," Luke said. "He was with us when we first discussed stealing the painting."

"Oh, but of course he should help steal the painting. His position at the gallery makes him invaluable. But for the forgery? No one has to know except you and me — and our wealthy buyer, of course."

Luke looked down at his beer, swilling the amber liquid in the stubby to froth it up.

Dipper would never agree to returning a fake to the gallery. There was absolutely no way. Steal the painting, demand arts funding — that was as much as Dipper would ever agree to.

But returning a forgery to the gallery? That was a stroke of genius. And to fool all those conservators and experts. To hang a fake in the gallery and *get away with it*? Well, that was pure brilliance.

Luke shook his head, though.

"Dipper will have enough of a problem with just stealing the painting."

"But he likes the idea of bringing the *plight of poor artists* to the public's attention?" Real said, a sarcastic tone underlying his words.

"Yeah. He really does. So I think he'll do it with us. But if he finds out about the fake," Luke pressed, "I'm just not sure what he would do. He might go to the cops. I can't say."

163

"In that case, I will arrange some insurance," Real said. "If there is any trouble when the deal is sealed, I will find a way around this. And he needs money, no? That can be arranged if necessary. Whereas you" — Real's expression lightened up then, broke into another sly grin — "I think you like the idea of sticking it to the establishment."

And Luke laughed. Because Real was exactly right.

Luke couldn't care less about the money.

It was the fuck-you that he liked the idea of. The fuck-you and the fuck-it, all rolled into one master stroke that would end up on the walls of the National Gallery of Victoria.

That had appealed to Luke very much.

At 12:15 that Sunday morning, Real led Luke back through the gallery and into his office, Dipper trailing behind them this time.

Dipper had driven them there from the pub, one hand on the steering wheel, the other engaged with a cigarette throughout the entire drive.

Luckily Luke liked the smell. It reminded him of when he was little and his parents would light up, the smoke wafting into the backseat. Cigarettes always smelled better to him in a car than anywhere else.

"So, what was so important that it couldn't wait until morning?" Real said as he sat down at his desk. "For heaven's sake, it's past midnight. Don't you boys sleep?"

"The cops are onto me," Dipper said, his hands fidgeting, restless without their constant cigarette companion. "They keep interviewing me, asking what I know, going over my story again and again. And now everyone's saying the painting's been offered for sale to a buyer in Adelaide," he continued, a bolshie tone slipping into his voice as he took out a cigarette and fitted it into his mouth. "And then you go to Adelaide, which, I don't know, seems like a hell of a coincidence. So I want to know ..."

And then he noticed *The Weeping Woman* resting against the wall of Real's office and stopped speaking.

He turned accusingly on Luke.

"I thought you said Real couldn't have taken it to Adelaide," he said, "because you'd stashed it somewhere."

Luke glanced over at Real and raised his eyebrows, hoping that the "insurance" Real had mentioned previously did not simply involve an offer of money, because by this stage Luke really wasn't sure Dipper would take that bait.

"It is," Real said and stood from his desk to clamp his hand on Dipper's bony shoulder. "It's stashed in a very safe place."

Dipper frowned.

"What? Right here? At your place? So you can take it to Adelaide with you whenever you want?"

"No," Luke said, realizing where Real was going with this. That it was time to tell Dipper about the fake. "In a different safe place."

Dipper squatted down and looked closely at *The Weeping Woman*, the vibrant greens and purples bright even in the darkened office.

"So what's this, then?" he finally said, turning to look at Luke.

"That's three hundred thousand dollars, right there," Real said.

Dipper stayed silent, looking at the painting, studying it.

"You did this?" Dipper said finally, looking up at Luke.

Luke nodded, running his tongue over his teeth.

Pretty good, isn't it, he didn't say. Because it was. It was absolute perfection.

"So you're going to sell a forgery to some poor sap for three hundred thousand dollars?" Dipper said.

"No," Real said, shaking his head. "We're not selling him a forgery. We'd have our legs broken if we sold him a forgery. And that's if he was in a *good* mood. No, we're giving this one" — he nodded toward Luke's forgery — "to the gallery. The Picasso we're selling."

All Dipper's skittish jittering stilled as this new news sank in.

"This can't be a surprise to you," Real went on calmly, returning to his desk and leaning back in the chair, folding his hands like a pair of gloves in his lap. "I'm an art dealer. I sell art. Did you think this was never going to come up? The chance to sell *The Weeping Woman*? You're jesting, of course."

Real had a point. His reputation preceded him. They'd both heard about the Whiteleys that were maybe not the real deal; the stolen Monet that was rumored to hang in the basement of some rich guy's house. If a person like Real suggested you steal a million-dollar painting, there was always going to be an angle.

"No way," Dipper said, stepping away from the two of them, separating himself from them. "This isn't what I agreed to. I'll go to the police myself. I don't care anymore if I go to jail for my part in it. This isn't happening."

Real puffed a snort of laughter out his nose, not even bothering to open his mouth.

"You will go to jail," he said calmly. "If you go to the police, that's exactly where you'll end up."

"Well, it'll be nice and cozy in there, won't it? With the three of us."

"Not three," Real said. "Just one. You."

Dipper looked confused.

Here came the insurance, no doubt. To protect Luke and Real from exactly a moment like this.

Luke swallowed, intrigued to hear what Real had in mind.

"You typed up the ransom letter on your old typewriter," Real reminded Dipper. "You handwrote the address on each envelope. It was an inside job, everyone knows that, and you're the man on the inside. It won't be the three of us. Just you."

Dipper looked from Real to Luke, then back again.

"If you go to the police," Real said, "I will simply explain to them that I, myself, am embarrassed and uncomfortable by the fact that you — a young artist who I have taken an interest in — approached me with the stolen Picasso, urging me to sell it to the highest bidder. I'll tell them that I tried to persuade you to hand yourself in, but that you threatened me. That I was scared for my life. When they do some digging — maybe with the help of a handy tip-off — they'll discover that you booked yourself into a hotel in Adelaide yesterday, apparently in an attempt to sell the painting."

"I've never been to Adelaide in my life," Dipper said, folding his arms around himself, looking boyish and uncertain.

"The Southern Star Hotel in the CBD says differently. Your name is on the register. Mr. Tony Di Palma, 52 Sycamore Street, Templestowe, I believe."

Dipper's leg starting jiggling again, his body as ever betraying his nerves. He took a fresh cigarette out of the pack in his top pocket.

"You're an arsehole," he said to Luke, turning away from Real.

"People don't even like the painting that much," Luke replied. "You've read the letters to the editor. Most of Melbourne thinks the painting's shit, something their grandkids could paint. They don't deserve it. Besides, they'll get a first-class forgery in its place. No one'll be any the wiser."

"Everything has gone exactly as you wanted it to go," Real pointed out to Dipper. "Arts funding has increased. You've raised the profile of *The Weeping Woman*. More people have gone to see the space on the wall where it used to hang than went to see the painting itself in the year or so since the gallery bought it. What does it matter if the painting that's returned is a forgery? It looks exactly the same. For all intents and purposes, it *is* exactly the same. Look at it." He nodded over at the forgery like it was a favorite child. "It's perfect. The back of it, everything about it, is exactly the same as the original."

Luke moved closer to the painting. He didn't trust Dipper not to put a foot through it at this stage.

"So you see," Real went on, "your concerns about the people of Victoria missing out on their Picasso are groundless, because they will have their Picasso. It's like that question. You know the one. *If a tree falls in the forest but no one is there to hear it, does it make a sound?*"

"I can't believe you're fine with this," Dipper said, looking over at Luke.

"Mate," Luke said. "What's not to love? I can't believe you're *not* fine with it. It's the greatest fuck-you we can give to the establishment. It's sheer brilliance. The gallery thinks this is the real deal. We get some cashola out of it — three hundred thousand, a hunnie each. And if you thought steal-ing the painting was a big fuck-you, then how much better is it when we return a forgery?"

"You think they won't work it out?" Dipper said, shaking his head. "You think the gallery won't go over that with a fine-tooth comb?" He moved toward Luke's forgery. Luke's whole body bristled. "You don't think they'll figure out it's a *fake?*"

"It's already been given the thumbs up," Real said, lifting a shoulder in an unapologetic shrug. "That's why I took it with me to Adelaide. For my buyer's expert to check on how authentic it looks. He's given it his imprimatur. We just need to wait another week or so until the oils are completely dry before returning it. Meanwhile, my buyer is coming to Mel-bourne next week with his expert to take our lovely lady back with him to Adelaide."

Dipper shook his head, not answering.

"And now," Real said, going over to a wine fridge and grabbing a bottle of Champagne, "we celebrate."

It was as he forced the cork out with his thumb that the phone rang.

Real checked his watch. It was late. Very late for someone to be calling. Luke wondered if it was the buyer from Adelaide, checking that the deal was still on.

The answering machine picked up the call.

"You have called the Sartori Gallery in Melbourne," Real's recorded voice said. "Our office is unattended at the moment. Please leave a message after the beep."

Beeep.

And then the three of them listened to a frantic voice — a man's voice, speaking in a rush into the phone.

"Real, it's me," the voice said. "If you're there, pick up. I've left a message on your machine at home as well. I need you to come to Russell Street Police Station. It's Estelle. She's in trouble. She's done a very bad thing."

Luke looked at Real, his eyes widening.

Dipper didn't know names. He hadn't been privy to details. But Luke knew exactly who Estelle was. Estelle was Real's sister.

Estelle was the one who'd stolen the screwdriver.

The security screwdriver they'd needed to take the Picasso off the wall that night two weeks ago.

The last person they needed down at the police station — the only other person in Melbourne who knew exactly who'd stolen Picasso's *Weeping Woman* — was Real's sister, Estelle.

Real grabbed at the phone, his easy manner gone.

The Ex

She left my beautiful boy with her psycho mum.
She left my beautiful boy with her psycho mum.
She left my beautiful boy with her psycho mum.
She left my beautiful boy with her psycho mum.
She left my beautiful boy with her psycho mum.
She left my beautiful boy with her psycho mum.
She left my beautiful boy with her psycho mum.
She left my beautiful boy with her psycho mum.
She left my beautiful boy with her psycho mum.
She left my beautiful boy with her psycho mum.
She left my beautiful boy with her psycho mum.
She left my beautiful boy with her psycho mum.
She left my beautiful boy with her psycho mum.
She left my beautiful boy with her psycho mum.

"Was Diff at the party? Is that why you" — Penny put her
fingers up in sarcastic quote marks — "*had to go*? Because
Diff was going to be there? Is that it? Was he there?"

There was the slightest movement of Rafi's head. *Yes.*

"Good. Great. So? How was he? How was the *amazing Diff?* Did he even bother to talk to you, Rafi? Was it the best party ever? I really hope it was, because my son's I-don't-know-where, but at least you got to go to a party where Diff whatever-his-*fucking*-name-is was, so that's the most impor-tant thing, isn't it? That you got to see some arsehole who couldn't give a shit about you? Because you know what, Rafi?"

Not Fifi.

Not anymore.

Rafi.

"He's not even into you. It's so obvious, it's embarrassing. But that doesn't matter, because the main thing is wow, party, great. That's really fantastic that you had a party to go to. Because fuck knows, you wouldn't want to miss out on a party."

"Penny," Mick said, wading in. "She couldn't have known this was going to happen. He's probably fine. Her mum's probably taken him for a walk or something. They'll prob-ably come back any minute."

Penny turned on Mick.

"Oh, of course. That's it. Because everyone knows it's per-fectly normal to take an eight-month-old baby out for a walk well past midnight in the middle of winter. When it's, like, five degrees or something. Sure. Why didn't I think of that? There's nothing strange about it. Thanks, Mick. They're prob-ably off having a lovely time." She hit her forehead with the palm of her hand. "It's so obvious. I'm stupid, aren't I? Stupid, stupid, stupid, stupid," she said, hitting her forehead with the palm of her hand every time she said it.

She needed the police here, now.

What was taking them so long? She rang at least ten minutes ago.

Penny had already ripped every fingernail off with her teeth, right down to the skin. *Rip, rip, rip, rip, rip, rip, rip, rip, rip, rip.* Ten nails, gone, one of them bleeding. Good. Pain felt good. She deserved pain. Anything to take her mind off the huge panic inside her head.

She wished the bistro was open downstairs. She wanted Moritz here. He'd help. He'd know what to do. She trusted Moritz.

Fifi — Rafi — was bundled up on the couch, her knees up to her chest, her forehead resting on her knees, her arms wrapped around her legs.

Penny wanted to shake her. Yell at her again. Scream. Punch. Kick. Tear out chunks of her hair. She continued pacing the lounge-room floor instead.

She looked at *The Weeping Woman* propped up against the cushions on the couch. The stupid fake that Luke had done. All anguished angles and jarring colors. Taken off the mantelpiece and put on the couch.

She turned around.

"And just by the way," she said, looking for extra things to be angry with Rafi about. "I don't want you touching my things. Luke gave me that painting. What the fuck were you doing putting it on the couch?"

Rafi shook her head, which was burrowed in under her arms.

"I didn't move it. Mum did," she said to her knees.

Penny stopped her pacing and stared at Rafi. She felt a chill on her back, like ghosts were tapping at her shoulder. Vaguely, in her tumultuous brain, a terrible, terrifying thought started coming into focus.

"La Llorona," she said, turning to face the painting on the couch. "What does it mean in English?"

Rafi hesitated for a second before saying into her knees, "The crying one."

"Crying," Penny repeated, turning back to Rafi. "As in weeping?"

Rafi jolted at the word "weeping." She looked at *The Weeping Woman*. She looked up at Penny in shock. Horror spread across her features like oil on water.

"It's a whole different story," Rafi said frantically. "La Llorona is a horse-headed woman who wanders the riverbank. This painting is nothing to do with La Llorona. There's no horse head, no river."

And Penny remembered exactly what it was that Frau had said to her earlier that week when they ran into her after they'd been at the park.

Babies drown, she'd said.

Penny remembered thinking at the time, through her pity, through her guilt at her clumsy response (*Oh, I'd never let anything happen to him*, as if it was up to her), that at least Richmond wasn't exactly a beachside resort area.

The only water you'd find in Richmond was at the public pool and the Yarra.

The river.

La Llorona. Walking the banks of the river looking for children to drown. That was what Moritz had told her. That was what Rafi just said. That was what the legend was about.

Penny felt her brain scrambling, even as she knew she had to stay calm. A scream was winding up inside her head, making it hard for her to know what to do, escalating her panic even as she tried to rein it in.

The Yarra River.

"Oh, my God," she said, her hands up at her face as the contents spilled out — distorted, anguished angles, distorted colors.

She went over to the phone and picked it up.

Dialed 000 again.

Police.

And finally (finally, finally, finally, finally, finally, finally), at that precise moment, she heard a car pull up outside.

The police. They were here.

They'd parked under the cherry tree out the front. Two of them, clipboards in hand, came toward her.

She ran down the stairs, not waiting for the police to take the time it took to come up to her. Why weren't they running? This was urgent. Important.

"Have you found him? Where is he? What's she done with him?"

She wanted to rip their folders out of their hands to see what was written down. Find out everything. Everything they knew.

They were two young guys, probably the same age as her. One of them was cute, she noticed, and instantly felt sickened at her own despicableness.

The walkie-talkie of Handsome Cop sparked into crackling communication.

Penny tried to decipher what the operator was saying.

She heard words like "river" and "baby" and "hospital."

And "dredge."

Penny felt her entire being break in half.

"Call Luke," she rasped, feeling her voice shattering as she turned for the briefest of moments back toward Mick, who was coming up behind her. Mick. Frivolous, let's-have-fun, let's-go-see-a-band Mick. "In my Teledex. To meet me at the hospital."

Her little boy, her beautiful Joshie, in that freezing cold river. Under the weight of all that water, trying to breathe, struggling to climb to the surface, struggling for his mum. She could feel the suffocation herself, the lack of oxygen, the gasping for breath. She wanted to physically get away from her own body, to scramble out of her own skin, to get as far away as possible from herself, her revolting self who'd killed her own baby as surely as if she'd been the one to push him into the river herself.

The Artist

Before Real left to go to the police station, he pulled Luke to one side and said, "Take the painting. The copy. Take it — I don't know where. Then let's just wait and see what she's said. But I can't have that here, not in my gallery, not if she's said anything to the police. I can't afford the risk, in case they turn up here."

"What am I supposed to do with it?" Luke said.

Hot potato, hot potato.

"Take it. Put it … I don't know, Luke. Sort it out. Put it somewhere. Then go home. I'll call you as soon as I know what's going on."

For the first time since they'd stolen the painting, Luke had a very bad feeling about what was going down.

"That's not going with me," Dipper said, shaking his head at Luke's forgery when they got out to the car.

"I just need to get it home," Luke said.

"Looks like you'll be catching a taxi, then."

It was well past one o'clock by now. There was no traffic but lots of people walking around. The last thing Luke wanted was for a group of guys who'd had too much to drink to walk past and notice he had Picasso's *Weeping Woman* in his hands.

That was how paintings got damaged.

Or people.

"Come on, mate," Luke said. "It'll take you two seconds."

Dipper shook his head across the car. "I can't believe what a right royal fucker you turned out to be."

"You've always known I was a fucker," Luke said. "Where's the surprise?"

"But this much of a fucker? No, I had no clue. What's he making you take it for, anyway?" Dipper gave Luke a piercing look. "What's going on? Who's Estelle? This Estelle turns up at the cop shop and suddenly you've got to move the painting?"

"He's just getting antsy. I don't know what's happening. Look, how about this. You take me back to my place, we'll sit down, and you can tell me why we shouldn't do this. I thought you'd be cool with it. It's a lot of money. We were always going to tell you once the deal was done."

Dipper looked at him. "She's the one who stole the screwdriver for us, isn't she?" he said, his eyes sharpening as things started to come clear. "You said one of the cleaners was getting it for you. There's an Estelle who works at the gallery."

"Let's just go," Luke said. "We'll talk about it at my place."

"That's her, isn't it?" Dipper said, making no move to get in the car.

"I'll tell you what. You take me home, and I'll tell you everything. But we have to get off the street."

Dipper kept watching him, not moving.

"Seriously," Luke said. "We'll talk. Just open the car and let's go."

Seriously. There was no way Luke was giving up on the arrangement he had with Real. He just needed to get the painting back to his joint, and he'd sort things out with Dipper once they got there.

Just as they walked into Luke's house, the phone rang.

Dipper held onto the painting, refusing to let Luke touch it.

"This is becoming a bit of a habit with you," Luke joked. "Holding the *Weeping Woman* for ransom."

"You going to get that?" Dipper asked, ignoring Luke's attempt at humor.

"If it's Real I'll pick up. Otherwise, no."

They listened to Luke's recorded voice ask whoever it was to leave a message.

And then a man's voice came onto the machine.

"Um," he said, sounding like he didn't quite know who he was calling or why. "This is Luke's phone, I hope. My name's Mick. I've just been out with Penny ... seeing a band."

Luke looked at Dipper. Weird.

"Anyway, she asked me to call you. There's been an accident. Joshie's in hospital. She'll meet you there. I hope you get this."

Click.

Luke felt his night split, in that moment, into two distinctly different scenarios.

He needed to stay home and convince Dipper to go ahead with their plan.

He needed to get to the hospital to see if Joshie was okay.

It was like the universe was toying with him, a cat batting its paw at a mouse. *Whatcha gonna do, Luke?* the universe was saying. *Whatcha gonna do?*

"I'll take you," Dipper said, heading back out to his shitbox yellow Datsun 120Y, the painting still in his hand. "We'll try the Children's first."

They drove up St. Kilda Road. It was the most direct route at that time of the night to get from Luke's place in South Melbourne to the Royal Children's Hospital in Parkville, and it took them straight past the National Gallery of Victoria — the NGV. The scene of the crime.

Luke knew that if they walked up to the building now — if they stopped the car and walked up to the building — the water in the moat out the front would be littered with coins that people had thrown in as they made a wish.

He knew that the water wall at the front entrance would be cold to the touch. Surprisingly cold. He remembered when he first moved to Melbourne for art school, eighteen years old, standing at the water wall with the palms of both hands flat against the window, water splashing around his wrists. Knowing it was uncool, that it was a little-kid thing to do, but unable to resist.

He knew that at this time of night, all the lights would be turned off and it would be quiet inside.

He knew that the guards would have finished doing their rounds and gone home hours ago.

He knew that there probably wouldn't be anyone hiding in the toilets.

Stealing the painting had been stupid-easy.

Luke had ambled into the gallery a little before close of play on Saturday the second of August, wandered around, then hid in the toilets on the second floor while everyone else left the building and the place was locked up.

The gallery settled into an oppressive darkness — a bone quietness. There was the occasional groan as the building shifted and got comfortable.

Luke squatted on the toilet seat and drank his bottle of beer. Not that he really felt like a beer, but he figured it felt like a suitably subversive and irreverent thing to do to pass the time, and waited for, well, he couldn't even guess how long — hours — until he heard the door to the bathroom swing open.

Luke didn't move. He didn't breathe. Even the fact of him being there, not moving, not breathing, seemed like enough to give him away. His very presence, the blood inside him, the breath he was holding in his lungs, felt like a flashing sign illuminating the cubicle with the words, *Thief here, thief here!* pulsing in time with his thumping heart.

Torch beams lit up the room like Christmas, garish and bright, swinging into the corners — treacherous fingers of light clutching under the toilet door in an attempt to catch him by the ankles, grasping for someone just like him.

He imagined one of the guards standing stock-still on the other side of the cubicle door — listening, waiting — and then finally saying, *Who's in there?* Like a Jedi knight, feeling the Force.

Or another guard pushing against each of the cubicle doors in turn, the lightest touch, and noticing that one of them was locked. *Who's there?*

That was all it would take.

Luke closed his eyes, retreating to old childish habits. *If I can't see you, you can't see me.*

He heard a cough — a clearing of the throat as the door to the bathroom closed and the guards left.

Code from Dipper, giving him the all-clear.

A few minutes later, Luke climbed down from his squatting position on the toilet seat and emerged into the freshly de-guarded, de-torched room, his knees creaky from being bent for so many hours, moving like an old man.

He lifted his arms up into the blackness, feeling the stretch down his sides, under his arms, in his shoulders. Then he pressed the button on his watch to light up the numbers. 8:47 p.m.

Just over an hour before Dipper and the other guy went home.

Just over an hour before Luke would pull off the art heist of … well, not the century — the theft of the *Mona Lisa* by that Italian waiter probably took that particular cake — but definitely of the decade.

A little after ten, Luke sneaked out of the men's toilets and crept up the corridor, past the costume display cases of eerie full-length Victorian gowns on headless dummies, to the European gallery.

Tucked inside his satchel was a length of bubble-wrap, some brown paper, a ball of string and a security screwdriver. On his hands he wore traditional curator's gloves, to serve two purposes. One, protect the painting. Two, keep his fingerprints safely on the tips of his fingers, instead of all over the walls of the National Gallery.

As Luke turned the corner into the European gallery, the neon greens and purples of Picasso's *Weeping Woman* met his eye, vibrating with clashing energy beneath the green wash of the Exit sign.

Luke pulled the snake-eye screwdriver out of his satchel, not at all sure it would work.

A snake-eye screwdriver was not something you waltzed into a hardware store and picked up. It was the one thing that would nail this as an inside job, a specially designed security tool whose sole purpose was to prevent exactly what Luke was about to do. Steal a multi-million-dollar painting off the walls of the gallery.

It had a flattened head with two prongs coming out that corresponded perfectly to the double-holed screws attaching Picasso's *Weeping Woman* to the wall.

That was where Real's contact in the gallery — his sister, Estelle — had come into her own.

Estelle, who was down at the police station at the moment.

She worked as a cleaner at the gallery. She'd been there for years. Nobody there knew her except the other cleaners and a few security guards, because she worked in the dead of night, but she knew where everything was kept. Keys to security cupboards, security snake-eye screwdrivers, that type of thing.

She'd stolen it out of the security storeroom for them.

Luke carefully unscrewed each bolt. As he lifted the painting carefully down onto the ground, the heaviness of it finally made him grasp the seriousness of what he was doing.

This was real. This was, well, heavy.

He leaned the painting against the wall, then stuck a small white card neatly in its place — a small white card that read, *This painting has been removed by the ACT.*

It was exactly what galleries did. Put a small white card in the place of a piece of art if it had been taken down to conservation or was to be photographed or if it was on loan to another gallery.

This painting has been taken to conservation.

This painting has been removed for photography.

This painting has been removed by the ACT.

The ACT: Australian Capital Territory. Also, Australian Cultural Terrorists. It was an old joke — how most artists Luke knew referred to Bob Hawke and the rest of the Labor Party up in Canberra. And the Libs weren't any better.

Anyone who noticed the card would simply think the painting was on loan to Canberra.

Luke carefully took the backing paper off the painting, then jimmied it out of its cumbersome frame. He ran his torch over the back of the canvas.

There they were. The signature, the date, the stamps — the proof that this was the real deal — secret business most people never saw.

He traced his fingers over Picasso's signature, then turned the painting back around and looked at her.

The Weeping Woman. The purples and the browns and the neon greens. There was something about the painting that had always reminded him of furrowed fields — the Weeping Woman's hair with its thick comb-lines in the green; the brown shirt, again with neat furrowed lines; the greenness of her face.

Although it was a painting of despair, Luke always felt like this painting, of all Picasso's work to do with the Spanish Civil War, seemed the most hopeful. The black and flat gray of the background seemed to jolt the vibrant colors into life, and the lilac tears running down the woman's green cheeks, her purple lips, were the color of flowers. Everything about it said springtime to Luke.

Where everyone else saw agony and anguish, he saw beauty and renewal.

He carefully wrapped her in the bubble-wrap. He was really taking her. He was wrapping her up and taking her away from her home. It was the moment that felt most like regret to him.

He wrapped brown paper around her and tied her with string, picked up the heavy Renaissance frame and took it out to the corridor, where he reached up and hid it on top of one of the costume display cases.

And then he walked back down the corridor to the men's toilets and waited for morning, when the gallery was unlocked and opened to the public and Luke walked out through the front door with his heavy army-surplus woolen coat draped over his arm and the most expensive painting in the collection tucked in underneath.

Dipper drove them along Swanston Street, straight up the guts of the city.

Estelle was at the police station, for whatever reason, Luke didn't know.

And now Joshie was in hospital, for whatever reason, Luke didn't know, either.

Dipper took a left toward the Vic Market and then headed up along Flemington Road toward the Royal Children's Hospital.

Luke couldn't help feeling that somehow the two things were connected.

Estelle had given him the screwdriver to steal the painting.

He'd given the painting to Penny.

The painting Real had told him Estelle wanted rid of, because she believed it was cursed. Something to do with her little boy drowning.

And now Joshie was in hospital.

Surely that had nothing to do with him giving the painting to Penny. But he couldn't shake his sense of unease.

After he walked out of the National Gallery that Sunday morning, *The Weeping Woman* under his heavy winter coat, he took it back to his studio and checked that everything about his copy matched up to the original — the colors, the thickness of the lines, the quirks of the stretched canvas.

He flipped the painting to face the wall and spent careful days copying the signatures, the scrawled validations, the pen-and-ink markings on the back that were only revealed once the frame was off.

Then he stood looking at the true *Weeping Woman* for the longest time. Studying her. By the end, it was almost impossible for him to drag his eyes away. The more he looked, the more he'd seen.

Luke found this often happened when he looked at great artworks.

He couldn't understand people who walked around a gallery, looked at a painting for a couple of seconds, moved on to the next painting, looked for a couple of seconds, moved on to the next painting.

What did people get out of it when they looked at art that way?

This is a picture of a weeping woman.

This is a picture of a man walking down Collins Street during rush hour.

This is a picture of a man standing on an overpass with no one around him.

That was it.

But true art needed to be looked at. Every piece of work was like a conversation between the artist and the person viewing it. There were hidden meanings. Secret codes. And each person saw different things.

Even Luke and Real had seen different things.

"Torrents of tears," Real said that day back at the bistro in Richmond when they cooked up the whole scheme. "Her eyes in their sockets are like boats tipping over from the volume of tears. You know the surrealists were fascinated by the theme of the eye staring out of its socket? With *The Weeping Woman*, her eyes are nearly sliding off her face, so much pain she's seen. And the sharpness of the nose, the angularity of the handkerchief. The way he scratched the lines of paint with the back of his brush. Everything about it is so raw and anguished."

But Luke didn't see raw anguish. Instead he saw beauty and hope and renewal.

And then a few days later, after checking and rechecking that his forgery measured up in all ways — back and front — to Picasso's, he took the painting around to Penny's house. He caught the tram there with *The Weeping Woman* unwrapped and in full view. The most conspicuous, most valuable, most stolen painting from the NGV collection on his knee, facing everyone on the tram.

It was basic-level bluffing. Hide something valuable in full view, and no one would see it for what it was.

He got a lot of comments, of course.

"I think someone's looking for that."

"Finally. You found it."

"That's one helluva reward you'll be collecting with that."

And Luke laughed.

The tram conductor came up to him all serious and said, "Is that what I think it is?"

And Luke grinned up at him and said, "Yeah, it's the missing two-million-dollar painting. But it's fine because I'm actually Pablo Picasso."

The tram conductor collected Luke's money, gave him his ticket and continued strolling down the aisle.

Luke sat and did the crossword. He carelessly left the painting on the seat beside him and nearly got off without it. The guy opposite him tapped him on the elbow and pointed at it.

"You don't want to leave without your masterpiece," the guy said.

And Luke laughed.

Because, no, he definitely didn't want to leave Picasso's masterpiece behind. He never had any intention of getting off without it. He knew exactly what he was doing when he stood up to get off the tram (apparently) forgetting to take *The Weeping Woman*.

It was basic-level Bluffing 101.

At Penny's, Luke made up some story that the painting was a copy he'd done for an exhibition.

"It's a lot smaller than the original," he told her when she said how realistic it looked. "There's a lot wrong with it, if you know what to look for."

Because rule number one in the bluffer's handbook was that people would believe whatever you told them.

If you told them it was a fake, they'd believe you.

Hiding the painting at Penny's place had seemed like such a clever idea. Hide it from the police, from Real, in the last place they'd think to look for it — in plain view on his ex-girlfriend's mantelpiece. It was Luke's way of keeping both himself and Real honest.

Well, as honest as a pair of thieves could be.

One for you, one for me.

Luke had always worried about Estelle's involvement.

"What's to stop her telling?" he asked Real when he first mentioned that Estelle would steal the screwdriver for them. "I mean, the gallery, the cops, they'll all know it's an inside job, because otherwise where we would get the exact snake-eye screwdriver from? What's to stop her from telling?"

"Darling," Real said calmly, "she won't tell anyone anything because number one, I'm her brother, and number two, she wants that painting off the walls as much as we do. She's the original Weeping Woman. Her little boy drowned when he was three and she's convinced La Llorona — *the Weeping Woman* in Spanish, a legend — was responsible. She's convinced that the painting is cursed. That it's tied to La Llorona. She's desperate to see the back of it."

Estelle sounded bat-shit crazy to Luke.

"But what about when we give it back to the gallery?" he asked.

"It'll be a forgery. I've told her that. Picasso's cursed painting will be gone, replaced by a harmless copy painted by you."

The Ex

Joshie's weeny body was wrapped up in space blankets and bear-huggers when Penny got to the Royal Children's Hospital with the police.

That was what the doctor called them. Space blankets and bear-huggers. Such sweet names for equipment so metallic and harsh.

"We're trying to keep him warm while his core temperature rises," the doctor said gently to Penny. "But it's tricky, because all that cold blood that has been at his extremities — his hands and feet — is now going back into his core, potentially cooling him down even further and putting him at risk of going into cardiac arrest."

Penny thought when she walked into the flat to find Joshie missing that nothing could have been worse.

But no. This was worse. Here in the hospital with her little boy lying on the bed unconscious — not asleep, unconscious — was worse. Being told that he might go into cardiac arrest.

He was a baby. He was too young to go into cardiac arrest.

She realized that she was moaning.

190

"Funnily enough, though," the doctor went on, "hypothermia can sometimes work in our favor. In order to preserve vital organs, the body shuts down, meaning less oxygen is required — there's less blood flow, and energy is conserved. So you have this situation where hypothermia can actually preserve the organs, because the organs don't need the same amount of blood as normal. The thing that's causing all these problems for your son is also the one thing that might actually save him."

When Penny first found out she was pregnant, she thought it was a disaster. It was exactly the sort of thing you didn't want at twenty-two years of age.

And when she told Luke, he didn't make her feel any better.

"What are you going to do about it?" he said to her.

"I don't know," she said. "I guess I thought we should discuss it. Work out what we're going to do."

Emphasis on *we*.

Luke shrugged his shoulders.

"It's up to you. I mean, I'm not ready to be a dad, but if you want it, it's your body. I can't tell you what to do with it."

"But it's your baby."

"Well, I don't want it, so get rid of it."

Get rid of it.

It.

Penny looked at Joshie's beautiful little face pale against the sheet, tubes and wires all over him.

She was over the eight-week mark when she went to the family-planning clinic on Church Street. They'd been great. No judgment. Practical, sensible, supportive.

"Having a baby isn't something to be taken lightly. You need to think it through. You have up until twelve weeks to make a decision. What do you do? Do you have a job? Are you at uni?"

"I'm at uni."

"Studying …?"

"Journalism."

"A baby makes study a bit more difficult. How long till you finish?"

"The end of this year."

She made an appointment to have an abortion. A "termination," the doctor called it. She was too young for a baby. She wanted to be a journalist. She was serious about her career.

She turned up at the clinic on the appointed day for her counseling session (she had to be counseled first, they'd told her on the phone, and then they'd make an appointment for her to have the "procedure") only to find a group of people picketing the front gate. Five of them. Standing out the front holding up signs saying *Unborn shouldn't mean unwanted* and *Speak up for those who can't speak for themselves.*

One of them was a girl her age.

Penny had read in the paper about protesters outside abortion clinics, but she hadn't realized until she was faced with them how intimidating they would be. How difficult it would be to walk through them with their placards and their chants.

She remembered feeling the redness rising in her face as she walked toward them. She'd barely come to terms with the fact she was pregnant, let alone going to have an abortion, let alone going to have to walk through a picket line so she could have her counseling session.

I'm not having an abortion, she found herself wanting to say to them, to those strangers. Those shamers. *I just want to talk about it. See what my options are.*

Right.

She shook her head, pushed fiercely through them and went to her session. Then she pushed through them again a little less fiercely, and as she walked home, she decided — for herself — that a baby wasn't as much of a disaster as she'd first thought it was.

She finished off her degree — a couple of credits, a couple of distinctions. Not bad for a girl from the country whose family had never been to university. But getting a job, a cadet-ship at a newspaper or a radio station or a television station when you were eight months pregnant? Doable? No.

She watched Joshie's beautiful baby face. A year ago she'd been all set to get rid of him. Now she couldn't imagine a life without him.

Whatever it takes, she thought to herself. *Whatever it takes to keep him alive, I'll do.*

Handsome Cop brought Penny a cup of coffee.

"I thought you might need this," he said.

"Thanks," she said, taking the hot mug in her cold hands but not bringing it up to her mouth. It seemed the least she could do. Not drink coffee in exchange for Joshie.

Whatever it took.

She didn't take her eyes off him.

"Your neighbor has turned herself in to Richmond Police Station," Handsome said, looking down at his own cup. "She says she was pushing the pram along the river and it fell in by accident."

Penny turned and faced him.

"That's bullshit," she spat, the fury that had overwhelmed her at the flat — the swearing, angry, pustular fury — grabbing at her face again. "She's a liar."

"They're going through everything with her at the moment down at the station," Handsome said. "Trying to work out exactly what happened."

"I can tell you what happened. She's *fucking crazy*. You can't trust a thing she says."

She knew she wasn't doing herself any favors by being so aggressive, but swearing was the only thing that felt right. The words on their own — *She's a liar, she's crazy* — they needed the "fucking" to give them some weight. Some gravitas.

"She says she can't swim," he said to her. Calmly.

Penny couldn't stand how calm he was. She wanted him to be as wound up as she was. But here he was, acting like Estelle's crazy bullshit story might actually be true.

"She says that's why she didn't jump in after him," he went on. "She says she was walking along and the pram slipped out of her hands. She says her hands were cold and they didn't have as good a grip as she'd thought they did."

"You don't believe that," Penny said. "You don't. You couldn't possibly. Tell me you don't. What about the guy? The one who saved him. What did he say? Who is he? Is he a friend of hers? He'll be able to tell you what really happened."

"He's not saying anything at the moment, I'm afraid. It's not looking good for him. At all."

Penny sat holding the full cold coffee mug in her hands. She wanted to explain to Handsome Cop why she hadn't drunk it, that it was a trade with the universe, a small offering to keep Joshie safe, but she knew it would make no sense.

She'd sound like she was the one who was crazy.

She wanted Joshie to wake up.

And then she heard someone behind her.

"Pen."

She turned around. It was Luke. Luke and Dipper.

Luke had come.

She put the mug down, stood up and put her arms around his neck, hugging him to her, her words tumbling out in a rush, trying to tell him everything, to tell him the whole story, the crazy bullshit story that Frau was telling, but that really Frau — Estelle, the neighbor — had pushed him in, that Joshie might die, that he might have a cardiac arrest, a cardiac arrest and he was only a baby, that she was sorry, that she should have been there for him, that she'd messed up.

That she was sorry.

The Artist

What? Just ... what?

Real's sister, Estelle, lived *next door* to Penny?

He'd left Picasso's *Weeping Woman* next door to Real's sister.

And she'd tried to drown his son?

What?

Luke could feel his brain repeating the same two things over and over, about Estelle, about Joshie, nothing clear, everything muddy and murky like the river Joshie had just been hauled out of.

The cops outside the hospital room hadn't mentioned Estelle, which was one good thing. Instead, everyone was talking about hypothermia. About Joshie having hypothermia.

Strangely enough, this was a subject Luke knew a bit about, from when he was growing up in Papua New Guinea.

People, he knew, thought you couldn't get hypothermia in tropical waters, but they were wrong. If the water was colder than your body temperature and you were in there long enough, you could get it.

His mum had been working in the hospital there, and one night she came home and told Luke and his dad about an old guy who'd been fished out of the water nearly unconscious. No one had been able to work out what was wrong with him for a couple of hours, simply because hypothermia hadn't occurred to them as Papua New Guinea was so hot and humid.

The guy nearly died, Luke remembered his mum saying.

And now Joshie was lying here, hypothermic. Because Luke had left *The Weeping Woman* at Penny's house.

Dipper tapped him on the shoulder. He'd been hovering by the door, giving Luke and Penny some space.

"I'm just going ..." And he motioned at the doorway with his head. "To the toilet," he added, his hand shaky as he pushed his hair off his eyes. "I'll be back in a sec."

Luke wanted to chase Dipper down the corridor, check that he wasn't leaving with the fake painting, that he was really only going to the toilet, but he had to trust that Dipper wouldn't do anything, wouldn't take advantage while Joshie was so sick.

"I don't get it," Luke said quietly to Penny once Dipper had gone. "Estelle pushed Joshie into the river? Estelle *Sartori?*"

Penny kept her eyes on Joshie, tearing up as she nodded.

"She's crazy. She saw the painting you gave me. You know, the fake Picasso, and I think that's what tipped her. She thinks a legend who coincidentally is called Weeping Woman drowned her son. Well, La Llorona, but anyway, Estelle deliberately pushed Joshie in. It wasn't an accident. I told the cops as soon as they showed up at my place, but I feel like they think I'm the crazy one."

Penny's face crumpled, and tears streamed down her cheeks. Luke put his arm around her shoulder and hugged her to him.

He needed to speak to Real — see what Estelle had told the cops. She could be telling them right now that the Picasso was in Penny's flat. That'd be one helluva get-out-of-jail-free card for her.

You've been arrested for trying to drown some kid, the cops might say to her.

Yeah? Well, you know that missing Picasso? she could be saying. *I just saw it, and for some strange reason it's in the flat next door to mine.*

He needed to get the painting out of Penny's flat before the cops turned up there.

And then he realized. The cops. Penny just said the cops had been round at her place. And the first thing they'd have seen was the whopping great Picasso on the mantelpiece.

Fuck.

He looked over his shoulder. Dipper wasn't back yet.

"What did the cops say when they came into your place?" Luke whispered to her.

"What?"

"Tonight? Did they see the painting?"

Penny looked at him, her eyes dragged away from Joshie for the first time since they'd both sat down at his bedside.

He laughed, as if it was no big deal.

"It's just that, you know, the last thing I need is to get arrested because they think that's the real Picasso you've got in your flat."

Penny blinked, as if her focus needed adjusting. As if she'd gone from short-sightedness to full twenty-twenty vision in that moment.

Dipper walked back into the room.

"Um, I'm pretty sure they wouldn't have cared less to see some crappy copy of *The Weeping Woman* in my lounge room," Penny said, her voice louder than Luke would have liked. "I think they were more worried about the little matter of my son, who was missing at that time. But no, seeing as you asked, seeing as it's so important to you" — her voice was rising in sync with her sarcasm level — "they didn't come inside the flat because they got the call on their radio just as they arrived. So luckily in all of this, the painting is still okay. Because in the end that's all that matters, isn't it? And then, of course, second, your son."

"Okay," Luke said. "Shh. Sorry."

"Did you just shush me? Don't shush me. Don't friggin' shush me. Our son is touch and go, and you're worried the cops might think the painting you gave me is the real deal?"

She shifted in her seat and looked at him full in the face.

"Is that right?" she said. "Have I got it straight? I just want to be crystal on this, because I'm hoping right now that I've completely misunderstood what you meant when you asked that question. I mean, if that's what you're worried about, a stupid painting, if that's your main concern, then, Jesus."

"Don't worry about it," he said, his voice as quiet as he could make it. "Forget it."

"You're such a dick."

She shook her head and turned back to face Joshie.

Luke put his arm around her again, but she pushed him away.

"Get off me," she said. "You've never been there for Joshie and me. Don't try to start now."

Luke heard Dipper quietly leave the room.

"Where are you going?" Luke said, grabbing Dipper by the arm as he walked down the corridor. "You can't just walk off. I'm coming with you."

"No. You stay here with Penny. And Joshie." Dipper's skinny body was ominously still — chiseled. No jiggling legs, no jittery hands.

"I'll come with you now," Luke said, "and we'll come back later. Penny's tired. She's upset. She doesn't want me here at the moment."

"The painting's at her place, isn't it?"

Luke hesitated, weighing up whether he could get away with lying. In the end, though, he knew Dipper had already guessed. He nodded.

"I'll tell you what," Luke said, keeping his voice low in the echoing hospital corridor. "How about we go back to her place, grab the painting and some of her things. Then you can bring me straight back here and we'll sort out what to do with the painting?"

Dipper puffed a laugh out his nose.

"What the fuck, mate?" he said, stepping back. "What the fuck is wrong with you? Your kid's in there and all you care about is the painting?"

Luke grabbed Dipper's arms with both his hands, facing him front on.

"I'll tell you what the fuck is wrong," he said, quiet now, right in Dipper's face. "We've got a two-million-dollar painting that will send both of us straight to jail if we get caught with it. My little boy's in hospital. I'm worried you want to double-cross me. So let me ask you something. What the fuck *isn't* wrong?"

Dipper wrenched his arms out of Luke's hands and pulled a cigarette out of his pack. He stuck it in his mouth, then took out his lighter.

"Okay. I'll tell you what," Dipper said through the ciggie. "I'll go grab the Picasso from Penny's" — he flicked his lighter and held the tip of his virgin cigarette to the flame — "and when things have settled down a bit, we'll sit down and discuss what we're going to do. The options being return the Picasso on Monday, or return the Picasso on Monday. They're your options. You'll notice they're pretty limited."

"How about this," Luke said, taking a breath. "I come with you now, we get the painting. I'll grab some of Penny's things, we work out exactly what we're going to do. We can't talk here. In a hospital. It's just … I need a beer. Let's go grab the painting and Penny's stuff, then get a beer and talk it all through."

Dipper looked down at the tiled hospital floor and dragged deep on his ciggie.

"Come on, mate," Luke said. "You gotta give me this."

Dipper kept his eyes on the floor, his Cheezel fingers gripping his fag.

"I don't have to give you anything," he finally said through a narrow mouth. "None of this is the way it was supposed to happen. I agreed to none of it. It wasn't supposed to be a grand theft where you then paint a forgery and try to return a fake to the gallery. It's not happening, Luke. I'm not letting it happen."

"Okay," Luke said, holding his hands up as if he could physically dam up Dipper's words and prevent them from spilling out onto the floor at their feet. "You're right. I fucked up. I don't know why I did it. Real convinced me. It seemed like a good idea, a fuck-you, but you're right. I shouldn't have done it. We'll give the painting back. Just let me go get Penny's keys and we'll go back to her flat and grab the painting together."

Dipper blew out smoke and shrugged. He looked tired. Too tired to argue. Luke could feel, in that moment, that he'd won.

"Okay," Dipper finally said, taking a long drag of cigarette smoke into his lungs. "I'll wait."

Luke went back to Joshie's room, leaving Dipper leaning against the wall like some length of pipe a builder had left behind.

"I'll go get some stuff for you," he said, leaning down beside Penny. "Clothes or whatever. You're upset. I'm sorry for asking about the painting. I just, I don't know, there's a lot of stuff going on, and I was … forget I mentioned it. You wanna give me your keys? I'll be back in twenty minutes."

Penny didn't say anything.

"Actually," he said, remembering, "the pot plant. Your key's still in there?"

She shrugged. The slightest movement of her shoulder.

Luke patted Penny on the arm. Friendly. Calm. No stress.

And then he thought of something. A small something nudging at the edges of his memory.

That day Penny moved into her new flat, Dipper had been there. He'd been helping.

Penny stood at the front door with the spare key in the palm of her hand, tossing it in the air, wondering what to do with it.

"Maybe you should have it," she said to Luke, offering it to him.

He knew what she meant by that.

"Nah," Luke said. "Just put it in a pot plant or something."

But Dipper said, "You can't put it in a pot plant. It's the first place someone would look."

"I'm a country girl," Penny had said to Dipper. "I find the whole concept of locking my front door bizarre. It'll be fine in the pot plant."

There were two people who knew where Penny left her spare key. Luke. And Dipper.

Luke ran into the corridor.

Dipper wasn't there.

Luke caught the lift down to the ground floor and ran out the front doors of the hospital onto Royal Parade.

Dipper's shitbox yellow Datsun 120Y?

It was gone.

LETTERS TO THE EDITOR
Monday, August 18, 1986

Cultural backwater
Melbourne! Melbourne! Melbourne! Whenever you make ignorant comments about kindergarten children being capable of painting a Pollock, a Braque or a Picasso you only prove what the rest of the world already suspects — that you're a cultural backwater.

Tony Sargood, Oakleigh

Condemned by ignorance
The destruction of the defenseless city of Guernica by the German air force in 1937 was the first blitzkrieg in modern warfare. *The Weeping Woman* is a universal symbol for the anguish of war, the loss of loved ones. All those who mock Picasso's work of art are condemned by their ignorance.

Lizzie Lambert, Prahran

Expensive save
Fear not, Mr. McCaughey. The most attractive part of that painting — the frame — was found intact. With any luck *The Weeping Woman* will never be returned and you can use the frame for something more worthy.

Glen Walsh, Middle Park

The Aftermath

The Ex

He was going to be okay.

Joshie was going to be okay.

"His renal function is good," the doctor said, flipping through the pages, scanning, impatient to skip to the good parts. "He's producing urine, his heart rate is coming along. He's starting to fight against the ventilator, so we're going to reduce his sedation, let him start breathing on his own and take the tube out of his throat. We'll keep him in a couple more nights for observation, but then, all going well, you can take him home. So for now, the best thing you can do is go home, rest, get yourself sorted out. He's going to be okay."

Penny burst into tears.

"It's been a tough couple of days," the doctor said, sitting down beside her and looking into her face. "Do you have someone who can take you home?"

Penny looked over at Joshie lying in the bed. Renal function good. Heart rate coming along.

She always called Luke her Bastard Ex, but she didn't really believe any of it. Not the Bastard part, and not the Ex part, either.

But now, sitting in the hospital with the kind-faced doctor asking if she had anyone, she realized that both the Bastard part and the Ex part were absolutely spot on. Maybe they were the only true things in her and Luke's entire relationship.

He'd said he was going to be twenty minutes, and then didn't bother coming back.

In a perverse way, the more badly he treated her, the more important she felt. She thought she was showing him how much she loved him by taking his shit.

The hint of other girls, nights when he didn't come home.

It felt like he'd been testing her over and over again, and if she got it right, if she managed to handle it in just exactly the right way, one day he'd turn around and say, *You know what? You really love me, I can see that. You've done everything I could possibly expect from you. You haven't given up on me. You've seen who I am underneath. You know how awful I can be, but you've proven yourself to me. You're the girl for me. You're amazing.*

And the orchestra would swell and the credits would roll. And what kind of idiot was she, living in a fantasy land like that?

Maybe if she had done things differently …

Maybe the first time she walked into the studio and he had a girl there, painting her, she should have said to him, *That's uncool. I'm not happy about this. It looks to me like you might sleep with her. And I'm not okay with that, because I'm your girl and you're my guy, and if you don't want it to be that way, then maybe we need to split up.*

She should have stood her ground. Stood for something.

But she never did. Because she didn't want to break up with him. Didn't want to be a nag.

Being with him some of the time was better, had been better, than not being with him at all. That's what she told herself in those days, anyway.

Besides, it wasn't definite that he was sleeping with those other girls.

Yes, it was. She knew he was.

Even before that last time, when she walked in on that younger version of herself, she knew he was sleeping with the other girls. But she pretended to herself that maybe he wasn't, because it seemed easier that way.

It was funny how you, yourself, could pretend something to you, yourself, that you, yourself, knew full well was untrue.

The machines that were monitoring Joshie beeped and dotted. The heart monitor graphed his progress across the screen, juddering up toward the top every few seconds, then back down to the bottom, then juddering up again, then dropping back down, exactly as it should.

If Penny was hooked up to that machine, her heart would show that same beeping graph across the screen, looking for all intents and purposes like every other heart.

Hearts didn't really break. Hers worked fine. Did its job. Pumped blood around her body. Did exactly what it was meant to do.

She was going to be fine.

She was going to be fine without Luke.

The Artist

It took Luke a while to get to Penny's flat from the hospital. There weren't any taxis, and he had to walk to Lygon Street to have any chance of getting one.

When he arrived, he went straight to the pot plant outside Penny's door and dug with his fingers in the dirt for her spare key.

The key was there. That was the first good thing.

First and only.

When he got inside Penny's flat, he looked everywhere — in every single room, in every cupboard, under the couch, under beds, everywhere — for *The Weeping Woman*.

She was nowhere.

Luke sat down on the floor in Joshie's bedroom, his back against the cot.

It was a nice room. Sweet. Happy.

On the walls were a couple of the paintings he'd done of Penny when they were together. In one of them she was sitting in a tree, her belly full of baby, her feet dangling down, the branches bare of leaves. In another she was in the shower, her back to him, the curve of her back beautiful, her hair piled up on her head as she shampooed it.

The one in the shower was an early painting. When he'd been in love with her.

The one in the tree, the pregnant one — her sitting big and fat with nothing, not even leaves, for comfort — had been when he'd fallen out of love.

The paintings Luke had done of Penny over the past couple of years charted his feelings for her like a surveyor mapping out a coastline.

The first painting he'd ever done of her, that first night back at his studio, he'd drawn the perfect beauty and incredible lines of her. Her hipbones, her concave belly, her long legs, her graceful neck. The candles he'd placed on the floor and on the arms of the couch flickered golden light over every inch of her body and face.

It was a portrait overlaid with sex and its knowingness.

Then there were the paintings he'd done as they spent more and more time together. Her laughing, sometimes shy, sometimes showing off, naked, dressed, in the shower, asleep with a blanket pushed off her body, her eyes closed, her hair mussed, reading, drawing. Everything she did, he documented and was endlessly fascinated by.

He had wanted to know everything about her. Every inch. What she thought. What made her laugh. What made her angry. What made her insecure. What made her her.

And then she told him she was pregnant.

She said she hadn't meant to get pregnant, but Luke found it hard to believe. This was the 1980s, not the 1950s. It wasn't like the pill hadn't been invented yet.

She made an appointment to get rid of it but then got spooked. Said she'd changed her mind, it didn't feel right. She decided to go ahead and have the kid.

He started painting Venus flytraps. Bear traps. Spider webs.

He painted Penny with a voluminous belly taking up the bulk of the canvas.

In a leafless tree. Alone. Legs dangling.

Tangled in an all-encompassing fishing net, her pregnant belly full.

She'd set him up. Trapped him.

She wanted to get pregnant, and there was nothing he could do about it. She was on the pill, but she forgot to take it sometimes, she said. It wasn't a hundred percent reliable, she told him. She'd been hungover one day and vomited, and maybe that was why it hadn't worked, she suggested.

But Luke wasn't able to shake the feeling that she'd set him up.

He started painting other women — whoever took his fancy. Whoever wasn't Penny.

He could barely remember now the Penny he painted that first night. The one in the golden glow of the candles. The one he couldn't get enough of. She didn't exist anymore.

On the wall opposite Joshie's cot, next to the painting of Penny in the tree, was a montage Luke had done for him. A face made out of a flattened-down VB can, two ring pulls nailed on as eyes, scraps of plastic for eyebrows, another nail bent down to look like a nose, the mouth a torn-off drink coaster.

He'd given it to Joshie as a house-warming present, kind of. Something for his new bedroom in Penny's new flat.

What sort of dad gave his four-month-old son a beer-face as a gift?

Luke remembered the day Penny said she was moving out.

"There's a flat in Richmond," she said to him. "Simone told me about it. It's got two bedrooms, and I've been to have a look at it, and I'm thinking it might be a good idea to move in there. You know" — and she shrugged at him — "take a break."

He looked at her in that moment when she said she was moving out, and for the first time in months he felt like he was seeing a vague semblance of the Penny he'd fallen for so heavily a couple of years back.

I'm not going to put up with your shit anymore, she was basically telling him.

But then she said she'd stay if he wanted her to. Told him she was sure it'd be fine if she called and said she'd changed her mind, Simone would understand. She didn't want to move out, not really.

And like a shower curtain sticking to his legs, Luke couldn't ungloop her from him quickly enough.

He looked around Joshie's room one last time. Then he went back down the hallway and through the lounge room, the painting nowhere to be seen.

He called Dipper's house. No one picked up.

He called Real's place. No answer.

He left to go and find Dipper.

The Girl

Rafi felt like that girl in the Boomtown Rats song.

The one who didn't like Mondays.

The one who planned to shoo-oo-oo-oo-oo-oot the whole day down.

Except, of course, Rafi wasn't planning on shooting up a school anytime soon. She didn't need to. She'd wrecked enough lives already.

People always said it was good to make mistakes. They said it all the time.

Make a mistake, they'd say. *It's the only way you learn.*

But it wasn't true. Not for Rafi. She'd made a mistake, and now she would regret it for the rest of her life. And others would regret it, too. For the rest of their lives, and other people's lives as well, in a big ripple effect created by her one mistake.

Mistakes were not harmless little bits of frippery that didn't matter. They weren't something that you dabbled in as you tripped gaily along the path of life.

Mistakes could be huge. Terrible.

Deadly.

She'd known it. She'd always known it.

All these years, she'd kept everything perfect. The lines straight, the colors coded. And now the one time she did something impetuous, something irresponsible, it had all gone to shit.

Rafi stood there with her hand on the answering machine, listening to all the messages that people had left her. Utterly, utterly stunned at how things had just gone from unimaginably bad to, somehow, something even worse.

Strangled. Speechless.

Rafi hadn't stayed at home the past couple of nights. She stayed at Uncle Morrie's place instead.

But this morning, this Monday morning, he told her they needed to go back to Cherry Tree Lane to sort out a couple of things.

"I'm going to grab some things for Penny and take them in to her at the hospital," he said. "And I'm going to take some things in to your mum as well."

The last thing Rafi wanted to do was go back to that flat. Ever.

By now people knew what had happened. That her mum had pushed a baby into the river and it may or may not have been an accident. Rafi hadn't seen the newspapers. Uncle Morrie said they didn't need to worry about what the papers said. It wasn't important. Journalists always got it wrong anyway. But Rafi didn't need to see them to know what the headlines would be saying.

Crazy lady tries to drown next-door neighbor's kid in Yarra River.

Daughter supposed to be babysitting but left to go to a party, leaving crazy mum in charge.

Baby might die.

Joshie. Might. Die.

Rafi was barely able to drag her feet into the flat, the oppressive weight of her mum sucking all the air out of its rooms.

Uncle Morrie went into Rafi's mum's bedroom and started getting whatever it was he thought she might need while she was down at the police station.

Rafi couldn't help seeing her mum sitting on the couch looking up at her, deciding whether to babysit Joshie or not.

"Well, I shouldn't …" her mum had said.

And Rafi had convinced her. Persuaded her. Begged.

I'll do anything, anything, if you'll look after Joshie for me just for a couple of hours.

Rafi wanted to change things, switch things around, *not* go in and tell her mum about the party, *not* worry about Diff Cameron, *not* go with Frenchie to the party.

Not make such a mess of things.

What time will you be home? her mum had asked.

And Rafi had run over and hugged her. Hugged her mum. Because she thought that her mum agreeing to babysit was about the best thing that had ever happened to them.

That it meant her mum was softening. That she wasn't resentful anymore that Rafi had lived while Tonio had died. That she'd painted La Llorona out of her system.

But that wasn't the case at all, as it had turned out. La Llorona was still in her mum's system, swilling around like sewage.

Rafi walked through the lounge room into the kitchen. She wasn't able to bear looking at the couch another second.

She went to get a drink of water. Not because she was thirsty, but because it would give her something to do.

On the kitchen bench, the answering machine was flashing.

Rafi looked at it. Twenty-seven new messages.

Yep, everyone had heard that her mum was a certifiable crazy person.

Uncle Morrie came into the kitchen and leaned against the kitchen bench, his arms folded across his chest.

"You know what," he said. "I don't think you should go to see your mum because you have a duty to her, or because she's your mum, or any of that crap."

Rafi looked at the red light on the answering machine, noticing that it was blurring as her eyes filled up with tears again.

"She's always been a shit mum to you. That's my opinion. She never stopped thinking about Tonio long enough to look up and see what she had right in front of her. And to be honest, I don't want to go in and visit her, either. But the way I see it, you've got two ways of handling stuff in life — the shitty stuff, I'm talking about.

"One: you handle it, you deal with it, and you move on, changed but better somehow for it. You can't know how it's made you better, but you have to believe it has, because otherwise you've gone through all that pain for nothing. Whether it makes you a better person or not isn't the point. Believing that somehow you get something good out of it, that's what matters. That's one way to deal with shitty stuff.

"The other way is to resent it, to keep going over and over it inside your head, to feel cheated, ripped off, bitter. To hold onto it and never let it go. To feel like you've been targeted, that the universe has it in for you, that life isn't fair, that other people have it better, that people should feel sorry for you, that the world owes you, that you're a victim. That only once everyone else in the entire world has been paid back for what you've been through will you start to move on."

Her mum.

Rafi put her hands up to her eyes and rubbed the tears away. But like a cut that wouldn't stop bleeding, her eyes didn't stop weeping.

"I don't want to be harsh," Uncle Morrie said, putting his arms around her in a big safe bear hug. "I know your mum went through something awful. I don't have kids. I can't imagine how bad it was for her, though I do know that if anything happened to you I'd never get over it. The thing that makes me so mad is that she still *has* you. She lost Tonio, I get that, but she still has you. And she's never appreciated how lucky she is.

"So that's what I don't like. That's why I don't want to visit her. But I'm going. And I want you to come, too. This will knock you sideways. What she's done, it'll be hard to get over it. It's a shitty thing to find out about your own mother, that she's completely nuts. I mean, I knew she was unstable, but this? This takes unstable to a whole new level."

Rafi laughed through her tears. He wasn't wrong there.

"But I want you to come to the police station today, because … I don't know why. I just think it's important. It'll be hard, but the worst that's going to happen is you're going to see your mum in jail. That's it. She'll be sitting there, and there'll be police there, and she might now be completely loopy, not even trying to conceal it, but that will be the worst. You can deal with it. And I can't tell you what will be good

218

about going, but I think you should. I'll be there with you. We'll stay as long as you want and then we'll go."

Rafi wiped more tears away.

"I just think it's important, Rif Raf," he said.

Rafi nodded.

"And this," he said, stepping away from her, looking down at the answering machine. "This is something to get over and done with, too. It's not going away. You might as well hear what people are saying."

He pressed the button on the answering machine, and she started listening to message after message.

And all the messages said that Guy was in hospital.

Guy — the guy Rafi met at the party, the guy she kissed, the one who drove her home — was in hospital, and it wasn't looking good.

He was the one who rescued Joshie from the river. It didn't even make sense, but that's what everyone was saying.

Rafi looked up at Uncle Morrie now, panic strangling her voice so that she couldn't speak, couldn't explain who Guy was, why he mattered so much. But Uncle Morrie didn't need her to spell it out.

"You want me to take you to the hospital to see this fella of yours?"

Rafi nodded. Mute.

"I'll drop you off as soon as we've been to see your mum."

There was a clutch of reporters out in front of Russell Street Police Station, but they didn't take much notice of Rafi and Uncle Morrie. Just looked over, assessed how much of a story was in them, then went back to their cigarettes and their talking.

At the front desk, Rafi kept her eyes on the floor while Uncle Morrie explained who they were. Who they were there to see.

A man in a suit came over to them and introduced himself. Rafi listened to none of it.

She didn't want to know his name, didn't want to be here. Didn't want to chat. She wanted to get whatever it was over and done with, then get the hell out of here.

She wanted to speak to someone about Guy and find out whether he was okay.

"A horse head has been found in a rubbish bin. Made of papier-mâché."

Rafi looked up at the man, startled.

A papier-mâché horse head. The horse head Rafi had bundled up and left beside the front door ready to throw out. Her mum had used it to live the La Llorona legend.

"The doctor's been to see your mother this morning and has given an initial diagnosis of a delusional disorder," he went on. "Apparently she never quite got over your brother's death, and for whatever reason, something's triggered a response where she's gone a bit deeper into her imaginary world than ever. It's hard for her to know what's real and what's not."

Rafi looked back down at the floor.

"Anyway," he continued, "it will be good for her to see you. To see both of you. She's down here." And he led Rafi and Uncle Morrie through a locked door at the side of the front desk and took them down a long corridor and through to where her mum was.

Her mum seemed exactly the same as always, which was perhaps the scariest thing of all for Rafi. She'd been living with someone who was completely nuts, but because she was so used to it, she hadn't recognized it.

"Tell them it was an accident," her mum said, her Spanish gaining speed as she spoke. "Tell them. You left me with him, Joshie, because you knew I'd keep him safe. La Llorona, she followed me here, to Australia. Tell them it was an accident. He was crying, and I took him to the river for a walk.

"I was called to the river. By La Llorona. She did this. She did this to me. She's been following me all my life. Tonio. This little boy. La Llorona did this, not me. Tell them about La Llorona. They think I've made her up. But you know she's real."

Her mum's voice dropped, sounding calm, reasonable, sane.

"You were there," she said, grasping Rafi's elbow. "In La Paz. He was your brother. I took him for a walk because he was crying. The pram came out of my hands and went into the river. It was La Llorona who took him from me."

Her mum had been pushing Joshie along the riverbank with a papier-mâché horse head on her shoulders.

Her mum was insane.

As they were being escorted from the police station, the same man who had led them in told them that Joshie was going to be okay.

He was being taken out of the induced coma.

He was going to be home in the next day or so.

Rafi burst into tears.

Uncle Morrie hustled her down the steps, unnoticed by the journalists.

Joshie was going to be okay.

She didn't ask about Guy. The cops would know if he was okay, but she didn't ask because she was so relieved about Joshie. She looked back at the doors of the station, thinking for a moment that she might go back in, but she didn't want to risk the journalists asking her questions, because questions from journalists weren't something Rafi felt strong enough to answer.

"Do you want to go and see Penny?" Uncle Morrie asked her. "See Joshie?"

Rafi shook her head. "Uncle Morrie. Penny hates me."

"Rif Raf, she doesn't hate you. Of course she doesn't hate you."

"No," Rafi said, a steeliness coming into her voice. "Joshie's going to be okay. That's all I needed to know. But I want you to drop me off at the Alfred. I need to see Guy. I need to be there."

Uncle Morrie kissed her head.

"Of course," he said. "Whatever you need, Rif Raf."

The Guy

A blue manila-type folder was hooked over the rail at the foot of the hospital bed.

Two people sat in straight-backed chairs beside his bed. The woman occasionally stroked his forehead, pushing his hair back. The man put his arm around her shoulders every so often, as if that was the only positive thing he could do in the circumstances.

The guy in the bed didn't move.

Didn't register any of what was going on around him.

The guy in the bed was him. Was Guy.

Guy looked down on the room from his position up high, but he didn't feel panicked or anxious. He felt an unutterable peacefulness as he looked down. He felt like he was up around the ceiling, but also so much higher than that. He felt the vibrations of each person in the room: the high-pitched vibration of his mum, the strident pitch of his dad, the dull vibration of his own inert body.

There was a hissing in his head, white noise, but his perspective was of everything. He saw everything perfectly. He had absolute clarity. Not just about the room, but about the whole situation.

He knew that his name was written on the front of the blue folder, in the nurse's surprisingly childlike handwriting. His address was there, his date of birth, the date of his admission.

He knew that inside the folder was a chart of his progress. It showed the incremental increases in his core body temperature, the alarming drops. It detailed how many milliliters of what medication he had been given to maintain his induced coma and what responses he'd shown to stimuli.

He wanted to tell his mum it was all okay. That he was happy. He was fine. He wanted to tell his dad he was sorry he'd messed up.

But he also wanted to say none of it. Nothing mattered in the end. It was all just words. His parents were going to be fine.

The hissing in his ears was turning into a roar.

And then he was gone.

The Ex

One of the doctors came in and nodded at Penny, then went over to the other side of the bed and checked a couple of Joshie's monitors, rubbing the metal disc of the stethoscope against his coat to warm it up before putting it to Joshie's skin.

She heard someone behind her.

"Knock knock."

Knock knock.

Who's there?

Girl.

Girl who?

Girl who went to see a band and left her baby alone with a psycho freak.

Penny pressed her hands against her eyes in an attempt to push her face back into some kind of recognizable form, then turned to see who it was.

Moritz stood there uncertainly, the height of him filling the doorframe.

Penny felt her face collapse in on itself. She put her hands up to hide her anguished expression, and then suddenly she felt Moritz's arms around her, holding her close, whispering into her hair.

"Oh, Penny," he was saying. "God. But he's okay, isn't he? Joshie. He's going to be okay. I've been calling the hospital constantly. I don't know if they passed on my messages." They hadn't. "Then I heard he was going to be okay. I had to come in and see you. I hope you don't mind."

"Are you family?" the doctor interrupted.

And Moritz replied, the words coming from down deep in his chest, rumbling against her face, "Pretty much."

"I need her taken home and taken care of for a few hours. You can bring her back later on this afternoon. She hasn't slept in two days. She hasn't taken her eyes off him. She hasn't even been out of that chair. He's fine, Penny," the doctor said gently. "He's going to be okay. But you won't be much good to him if you don't look after yourself. Can you do that for me?"

"Will do," Moritz answered. "That's what I'm here for."

"Rafi's been beside herself," Moritz said, keeping his eyes on the road. "Whenever I wasn't on the phone to the hospital, she was, trying to find out how Joshie was going."

Penny didn't say anything.

She didn't want to talk about Rafi. She'd never be able to forgive her for leaving Joshie alone with Estelle. What kind of person thought it was okay to do something like that?

Penny shook her head, as if physically trying to shake Rafi's name out of it.

"There's something you should know," Moritz said gently. "I don't know if now's a good time, but it's probably as good as any."

226

"There's something *she* should have known," Penny said, "and that's not to have left my son with her psycho mother. No offense."

Moritz laughed.

"You're right. And that's our fault, Real's and mine. We always tried to hide Estelle's craziness from Rafi. Of course, we didn't realize she'd do something like this — we never expected something like this — but we kept some of the bigger issues from Rif Raf. We just didn't want her to know. We thought that if we could keep her with her mum, that was all that mattered. But it wasn't right. We did the wrong thing."

Penny looked out the window. She didn't want to listen to this. She didn't want to hear how lovely "Rif Raf" was.

"Rif Raf" had nearly killed her son.

"When she told us things Estelle had done, we'd tell her it was normal. That plenty of mothers would do something like that. I guess we thought if she didn't pay too much attention to the craziness, it wouldn't affect her too much. Our aim was to get her to the end of Year Twelve, and then we thought she could move into university college and start living a normal life. She hasn't had a normal life."

Penny felt an anxiousness crush her chest, making her breathing shallow. She didn't want to hear any of this.

"A few years ago, we did suggest sending Rif Raf to boarding school. Real was happy to pay. We could see that Estelle wasn't coping with having a teenage daughter around the house, especially when what she really wanted was a three-year-old boy on her knee."

Penny could still feel the rawness of the feeling — the fear, the terror at the thought of Joshie not surviving.

She shook her head again.

"Rafi didn't want to board," Moritz said. "She didn't want to leave her mum at home alone. She felt like she was all Estelle had. She felt like if she wasn't there, the whole place would fall apart. She's the one who does all the cooking, all the cleaning, everything. She does everything for Estelle. I give her plenty of meals to take up as well, of course, but looking after her mum, that's what Rafi's been doing since she was a little tyke. Ever since her brother drowned."

Penny could feel her mouth filling with the tears she was refusing to let escape from her eyes.

"I don't expect you to forgive her," Moritz said, and Penny could feel the tears rolling down her face, her forehead scrunching. "But you need to understand what she's been through. She's seventeen years old. She's a kid. For once in her life, she messed up. And believe me, she'll never try anything like this again. She keeps telling me over and over that it's all her fault, that she shouldn't have left him home alone with her mum, that she knew it was the wrong thing to do, that she shouldn't have done it. The poor kid. I know you're angry with her, but I'll tell you what, my heart's just about breaking in two to think of how hard it must have been for her to take a risk, do something irresponsible, and then how badly it blew up in her face."

Penny thought back to Rafi cutting her hair the first few times. The shoulders hunched, the brow low in concentration, trying to get it perfectly right, even while Penny was telling her not to worry about it, to relax, that it was only hair, that it didn't matter.

"She shouldn't have taken a risk with Joshie," she said quietly. "You don't take a risk with someone else's child."

Penny looked away from Moritz, concentrating instead on the streets of Carlton skimming past her window.

They were turning right from Victoria Parade into Hoddle Street before Moritz spoke again. His hands were on the steering wheel, his eyes were on the road.

"There's something else," he said. "Something that … I don't know what you'll do once you hear it, but you need to know. And if you want to go to the police with it, you're well within your rights."

Penny looked at him, studying his profile as he watched the road.

"That painting in your lounge room? That was the real deal. That was worth over one-and-a-half million dollars — a genuine Picasso."

Penny looked back out her window.

She'd known. Inside herself, she'd always known. It was too good, too beautiful. It had an aura about it that you didn't get from a hastily painted copy of something, even something painted by Luke — even to an untrained eye like hers. She'd deliberately not looked at it too closely, didn't look at the back of it, because she knew that if she had looked, saw how authentic it was, she couldn't guarantee what she'd do.

Like everything else to do with Luke, she had deliberately looked away, even when she knew the truth down in her gut.

"I'd just got home from the bistro," he went on, "when Stel called me from the police station. When I arrived there, she was rattling on about it being an accident. That she'd taken him for a walk, Joshie, and the pram had slipped from her fingers. Into the river."

Penny felt fury welling inside her, having to listen to that bullshit story again.

"I don't believe her, if that's any consolation," Moritz said. "I don't believe it was an accident."

It was a consolation. It didn't help, but it was a consolation.

"As soon as I realized she'd done something to Joshie, I called Real and told him to meet me at the police station. I wanted to come find you. Make sure you were okay."

The lights at Bridge Road turned red. The two of them sat watching the road in front of them, its traffic passing them by in a crisscross.

"You weren't home, of course. You'd left already for the hospital. But Rafi was still there with Mick."

The last thing she'd said to Mick had been something along the lines of, *Stupid, stupid, stupid*, as she hit her own forehead with the heel of her hand.

Not her best effort.

Not even close.

"Mick left, and I took Rafi back to her place. An hour or so later we heard someone opening the door to your flat."

Penny had become distracted at the memory of hitting her forehead with her own hand.

"What?" she said sharply now.

"We thought it would be you back from the hospital, so we opened our door to ask you how Joshie was. But it wasn't you. It was some friend of yours."

Penny frowned.

"Luke?" she asked.

Moritz shook his head. "His name was Dipper. He said he was a friend of yours. That he'd just been with you at the hospital."

The lights turned green. Moritz put the car into gear.

"It seems Dipper was one of a small group of people who were involved in stealing *The Weeping Woman*. Along with your ex, my sister and my brother."

"Estelle? *Real?*"

Moritz nodded.

"Estelle works at the National Gallery. I don't know if you knew that."

Penny shook her head.

"She's a cleaner there. And my brother, he sells art for a living. I don't know if you knew that, either?"

Penny shook her head again.

"My brother has been involved in, shall we say, suspect art for a long time. That's why we moved out to Australia. I'd gone to Paris to stay with him. I was only nineteen, and suddenly we were up and leaving the country in the middle of the night, going to London, trying to buy tickets to Australia right there and then, because some guy from Texas was going to kill him. Sartori isn't our real name. Our real name is Wallechinsky."

Penny didn't answer. What did you say to something like that?

"Sartori was Estelle's married name. It seemed as good a name to take as any. The thing I'm trying to tell you is that Estelle stole a screwdriver to help them steal the painting. They wouldn't have been able to take it otherwise. I'm furious with Real for getting her involved, knowing how fragile she is, but he thought it might help.

"We both knew she'd started to spiral downward since the gallery bought the painting. She was talking about La Llorona again, saying La Llorona was in Melbourne, that the gallery should never have bought *The Weeping Woman*, it was bad luck, it was cursed, that type of thing. Because *Weeping Woman* translated into Spanish — "

"Is La Llorona," Penny finished for him.

Moritz smiled at her. A sort of sad smile.

"Correct. Another thing we kept from Rafi. Unwisely, I think it would be fair to say from this vantage point. Rafi had no idea it was this painting from the gallery affecting her mother. Time went on, and Estelle got worse and worse, until she began painting La Llorona again.

"So Real told her he'd get the painting out of the country — that was a lie, he was only sending it to Adelaide, but she would never have found out — and that she wouldn't have to worry about La Llorona anymore. And the thing was, it worked. Once *The Weeping Woman* was gone, as of the other week, she stopped painting. She perked up. It was like a cloud had lifted from her, and suddenly she was free."

Penny still didn't know what to say.

"But then she goes into your flat that night to babysit Joshie, thinking she's never going to see La Llorona again, and there was *The Weeping Woman*, cursing her from your mantelpiece. And it tipped her. She felt like she was being followed, that everywhere she turned, she saw La Llorona. It sent her, it made her, crazy.

"As soon as I saw Dipper come back out of your flat that night with *The Weeping Woman* in his hands, I knew that was what would have set Estelle off."

"So what happens now?" Penny said. "We call the police and get them to come round and pick up the painting?"

"Dipper and I returned the painting yesterday. Anonymously. He was very intent on giving it back, very anxious to go. Beside himself. As it turned out, Luke was on his way over to try to get the painting as well."

Luke. When he left the hospital, saying he was going to grab her some stuff. He was truly a Bastard Ex.

"I recognized him," Moritz went on. "Dipper. He'd been in my bistro before, a few months ago with Luke and Real for a long boozy afternoon. I began to realize that Real might be tied up in the whole mess … and possibly Estelle, too … so I told him I'd help him. And he told me everything.

"We put the painting in a locker at Spencer Street Station and posted letters earlier today to the TV stations — they should get them tomorrow — telling them to search locker 227 for it. Real knows. He's not happy about it, but that's not my problem. He shouldn't have done it in the first place. And now it's up to you whether you go to the police or not. It's out of my hands. Your call."

Penny looked back out the passenger window.

She was as guilty as any of them in a way. As soon as Luke turned up with the painting, she should have checked it out, called the police. But she didn't want to dig too deep, didn't want to admit to herself that it was the missing painting, because Luke had given it to her.

It made her feel special.

And Luke was right. It wasn't everyone who could say they had a one-and-a-half-million-dollar painting by Picasso propped up on their mantelpiece.

If she went to the police, a lot of people would go to jail: Luke and Dipper and Real and Moritz and Estelle, and maybe even her. Because, come on, as if the cops wouldn't wonder how it came to be that she had the painting on her mantelpiece for two weeks and never once thought to check the back of it.

233

Moritz pulled the car up in the front of the flats. It was a relief to see their white balconies again, the cherry tree pushing up the bitumen.

She doubted she'd tell anyone. The story of the year, and her an aspiring journalist. Keeping her mouth shut.

Moritz turned in his seat to face Penny.

"But in the end, all of that pales into insignificance compared with my next big question … how did the date go?"

And for the first time in a very good while, Penny laughed her head off.

234

The Artist

It was Monday afternoon, just after three, when a shitbox yellow Datsun 120Y finally drove down Dipper's street and parked out the front of his house.

Luke got up from the curb.

"Tell me the Picasso's in the boot," he said, opening the passenger-side door and leaning in to face Dipper.

"The Picasso's in the boot," Dipper said, his hands splayed like he was trying to catch the shit that would otherwise have been about to hit the fan.

"The forgery, too?"

"Forgery, too."

"Oh, thank fuck," Luke said, running his hand over his face. "Okay. We need to talk. I've tried to call Real, but he's not answering. Have you heard anything? Where have you been?"

Dipper looked at him. "Driving. Thinking. How's Joshie?"

"I don't know, mate," Luke said, a snappiness clipping at the heels of each word. "I've been chasing all over Melbourne trying to find you, haven't I?"

Dipper frowned. "You've been waiting here the whole time? You didn't stay with Joshie?"

"Well, yeah, I couldn't, because I was waiting for you. I've been shitting myself that you'd done something stupid with the paintings. If you'd come home, then I could have gone back to the hospital and been with Joshie. So, thanks for that," Luke said. "Jesus, you had me scared. Everyone says I'm a wild card, but you, mate, you make me look like a friggin' amateur."

Dipper pushed his hair off his face, then grinned at Luke.

"Well, I might as well show you," he said, getting out of the car and walking round to the boot.

"Show me what?"

Dipper stood at the boot and waited till Luke joined him. And then, ceremoniously, he opened it up.

E. M. P. T. Y.

Luke looked at him. "Where are they? You said they were in the boot." He wasn't quite sure what this game was.

"No. You *told* me to tell you they were in the boot. So I did. But no, they haven't been in the boot since I took them out this morning."

Luke looked at the empty boot.

"Your one," Dipper said, "your version, you can have back. I kept it for you. Although it's not worth half as much as it was. Not with that massive tear it's got down the middle of it."

Luke didn't say anything. What was there to say?

"And Picasso's much superior version? Well, they'll find that soon enough. Sometime tomorrow, I'm estimating. Which leaves you free to go to the hospital and find out how your son is going."

Dipper pulled a cigarette from his pocket and poked it into his mouth, then pulled out a box of matches and struck one against the flint, holding the flame up to his face.

Only the barest shaking of his hands betrayed him.

"And this?" he said, pointing at his own chest, then Luke's chest, then back to his own. "This friendship thing we had going?"

He flicked the match on the ground between their feet.

"This friendship thing is over."

The Girl

Hospitals, as it turned out, were very strict about who could see their patients.

They wouldn't let just anyone in, especially when the patient in question was so sick — as sick as Guy.

"I'll wait," Rafi said when the nurse told her she couldn't go in.

"But it could be days."

"I don't care."

A little while later, a woman came over to Rafi. She was older than Rafi's mum, but somehow younger-seeming, with a friendly face.

She sat down on the bench next to Rafi.

"I'm sorry," she said, "but do I know you? Are you one of Guy's friends?"

"Is he okay?" Rafi asked.

The woman looked down at the floor and shook her head.

"We're still waiting to see. He's awake now, thank God, but he's not … I'm Guy's mum. I apologize, but I don't remember you."

Rafi frowned.

238

"I'm a sort-of friend," she said carefully.

She wasn't *exactly* a friend of Guy's. "Friend" had different connotations than what she was to him. Or at least what he was to her. What had happened between them.

"Sort-of friend" was a much better description.

The woman looked at Rafi thoughtfully.

"Were you at the party?" she asked.

"Yeah."

"He was driving you home, wasn't he," his mum said. It was a statement, not a question.

Rafi nodded.

"Tell me what happened," his mum said, bending down so she could sneak a look in under Rafi's eyelashes. "I need to know how he … what happened that night."

Rafi looked down at her hands, guilt bringing a hot blush to her face.

"Oh. Well, I was supposed to be babysitting …"

And then she looked at Guy's mum, seeing the deep, inconsolable worry etched into her kind, warm face properly for the first time, and she started to cry as she described the mess she'd made of everything.

"I was supposed to be babysitting Joshie, the baby that, you know, who Guy …"

His mum's eyes followed her face. She was nodding.

"But I heard about this party, and I wanted to go, so I got my mum to babysit instead. And I thought it would be fine. I didn't know that she'd …"

She couldn't put into words what her mum had done, because she wasn't sure what the right words to use were.

"Then he drove me home, and I thought he was driving straight back to the party," Rafi said, twisting her fingers

239

over each other. Middle over pointer. Little over ring. "But he must have seen … my mum, and … the pram … what happened, and … jumped in."

The older lady's eyes widened.

"That was your mother? The woman who pushed in the pram?"

Rafi nodded.

Guy's mum stood up and went back in the direction she'd come, without saying another word.

The Guy

Guy had amnesia.

And from the sounds of it, amnesia-world was a very good place to be.

He lay there feeling groggy, hearing that he'd had a party a few days ago. That he'd driven his mum's (new) car, crashed it, jumped into the river, saved a baby, nearly died, and had been in hospital for the past couple of days in an induced coma.

That the police wanted to talk to him about driving under-age, unlicensed and under the influence of alcohol.

Ditto went for his parents. But also on their list were having a massive, out-of-control party at their house and forging his school reports.

"Not that I want to discuss any of it now," his dad said, "but when we spoke to the school this morning to update them on your progress, they told us a few bits and pieces that didn't quite measure up to our understanding of things. About your marks and whatnot."

Guy looked at him blankly.

This — the forging of his school reports — this he remembered. It was something he'd done ages ago, months

241

ago. But when amnesia has been handed to you on a platter, why not use it?

"Amnesia is a common side effect of hypothermia," the doctor said to them, standing by Guy's bed and picking up his wrist to check his pulse. "How permanent it may be depends on the individual."

Guy was pretty sure he was going to be an amnesiac for a very long time.

Maybe the rest of his life.

Guy's throat hurt.

He had trouble focusing.

He could hear his mum talking, saying something about "just turned up" and "waiting in the corridor" and "her mother" and the low rumble of his dad talking his mum down.

He moved in the bed, adjusting his body, getting comfortable.

"My throat's sore," he mumbled.

"That's from being intubated," the nurse said as she put a tiny glass of water on the tray by his bed, along with some custard.

Guy's dad looked like an identikit image of himself. He was all dark outlines and had a flattened, unfilled-in look to him. A frown arrowed down his eyebrows and pointed toward his nose. There was a gray lead-pencil texture to his hair.

And then, in direct inverse proportion to the wind-knocked-out-of-him vibe of his dad, Guy's mum looked all puffed-up and spongy, like she'd sucked all the moisture out of the room and filled herself up — especially around her eyes — with liquid.

242

His dad looked saggy, his mum looked baggy.

And Guy felt both those things at the same time.

He also felt overwhelmingly sleepy, even though he'd only just woken up.

Two days, they said. He'd been out for two days.

And the last weekend — he couldn't remember any of it.

Apparently he drove a girl home from his party, and on his way back he saw the baby being pushed into the river and jumped in.

It didn't sound like him at all.

He didn't like water. Didn't like the cold.

But even though his throat hurt and he felt so tired, so full-body bone-tired, he felt proud that he'd jumped in and saved a baby.

That was ace.

True, he couldn't *really* take any credit for it, seeing as he didn't remember any of it, but yeah, it was an ace thing that unremembered Guy had done.

He wondered who the girl was. Someone who lived in Richmond, he gathered. He didn't know anyone who lived in Richmond. He didn't think he did, anyhow. Most of his friends lived on the south side.

So who was she?

There was something intriguing, tantalizing about the idea of a girl who was good enough to leave your own party for, and to drive home in your mum's (new) car, unlicensed. But he didn't have a clue who she was. He might never meet her again. Unless she came up to him another time at another party and said to him, *Do you remember me? You drove me home from that party. I'm that girl.*

Then he'd find out what it had been about her that had made him want to drive her home from his party. Especially when he'd been drinking.

He thought of Rachel Henry and Stu Milford.

He could have killed her. This girl. This unremembered girl. Things could have turned out so much worse than they had.

"There's someone here to see you," his mum said. "She's been waiting for hours. I told her to come back another day, but she wouldn't leave. I don't know if you should see her. If you don't want to, I'll tell her ..." And she shook her head.

Guy wasn't sure he wanted to see anyone just yet. He felt warm and beddy. Pleasantly dopey. Whatever the doc had given him was kicking in very nicely.

"Who?" Guy asked.

"The girl whose mother pushed the baby in," his mum answered, a bitterness under her words.

Guy felt like he'd been slapped.

The daughter of the woman who'd pushed the baby in? Nope. He was pretty sure he didn't want to see the girl whose mother was enough of a fruitcake to push a baby into a river. The daughter was probably nuts as well.

"What's she want?" he asked. The drugs they'd given him were making his speech a little sloppy, a little slurry, so it came out, *Wa's she wan'?*

"She wants to see you," his dad said. "She met you at the party."

Guy frowned, having trouble working out the relationship. The daughter of the woman who pushed the baby he'd saved into the river was at the party? Was that right? Was that what his dad meant?

"I don' thin' …"

"That's okay," his mum said, sitting on the bed beside him and pushing his hair off his forehead, the way she used to when he was a little kid. "You don't have to see her. I'll send her away. I don't even know what she's doing here. She shouldn't have come."

"Bu' she was a' the par'y?" Guy slurred.

His mum nodded. The slightest tip of her head.

A minute ago, Guy thought he didn't want to see this girl, but he couldn't remember why anymore. She'd been at his party. She must be a friend of his.

"Yeah," he said sluggishly.

"Yeah, what?" his dad asked.

"Bring 'er in."

The girl walked into the room, and Guy felt a tug of something. She was beautiful, that was for sure. Long, thick dark hair and a mouth that he could have fallen for in a big way.

"Hi," she said.

"'ey," he said, grinning at her.

"Do you remember me?" she asked.

He shook his head.

"Wish I di'," he said, sounding like a dope. Sounding full of dope.

"You drove me home," the girl said. "From your party. I'm the reason you're in here. Otherwise you would have stayed at the party, safe."

Guy could feel his mum hovering. He could feel himself sinking into sleepiness, into the drugs that were in his blood, but he wanted to stay close to the surface, near this girl.

"Wha'?" he said to her. "You wha'?"

"I'm the girl you drove home. I'm the one — "

"He's got amnesia," Guy's mum said. Snitchy. Pissed off. "He won't remember anything from that night. I think that's probably enough now. He looks like he needs to go to sleep."

"No," Guy said, grabbing hold of the girl's hand. "Wai'. Thisis the girl," he said to his mum, words slopping. "This girl, she's th' girl." He stopped talking, drifting off. He shook himself awake. This was important. "Sorr'. I'm really tire'. Can you come back an' see me?"

The girl looked at him and smiled.

She had the most beautiful smile he'd ever seen in his life. He wasn't sure if it was the drugs, but everything about this girl was infused with something sparkly.

"Tomorrow," he said. "You come ba'?"

She nodded.

"Bu' hang on a sec," he said, feeling himself drifting off.

There was something he needed to ask her. A question. It was rising in his brain like a bubble. He had to ask her this one thing before she left.

"You're … rough. 's that right?"

She frowned at him. "Um. You banged my nose. At the party. Is that what you mean?"

"No. You. Your name — 's Ruff?"

"Rafi," the girl said, tears in her eyes.

"Raf," he repeated. "Raf."

He smiled.

And fell into the sleep of the deeply, deeply happy.

Still holding her hand.

Picasso's *Weeping Woman* was found in a locker at Spencer Street Station on Tuesday, August 19, 1986.

Rumors still abound that *The Weeping Woman* hanging in the National Gallery on St. Kilda Road, Melbourne, is actually an expertly executed forgery, while the genuine painting was bought by a wealthy businessman who has the painting stored in a basement for him to look at in his quiet moments.

But, of course, that's just a rumor.

ACKNOWLEDGMENTS

I'd like to thank the following guys, girls and artists who helped me write this book (no exes were used in the making of this book, because generally exes are bastards and best avoided):

Cat McCredie, Kim Kane, Susan Stevenson, Eliza, Holly and Simone Lambert, Alexandra, Lucinda and India Patterson, Danielle Binks, Leanne Hall, Fiona Wood, Will Kostakis and Andrew Williams for astute, honest feedback on early (sometimes very, very early) drafts.

Lewis Miller, Ashley Crawford, Mark Howson, Mark Schaller, David Larwill, Stieg Persson, Greg Ades and Roger McIlroy for the inside nod on the Australian and international art world.

The Australian Cultural Terrorists (whoever you are) for that little act of anarchy way back in 1986.

Full credit to Peter Greenaway for the title of my book — his 1989 film *The Cook, the Thief, His Wife and Her Lover* summed up the eighties for me. I hope he doesn't mind me commandeering his title for my own purposes.

The following books were invaluable in my research (and make excellent reading): *Picasso: Creator and Destroyer* by Arianna Stassinopoulos Huffington; *Fake: The Story of Elmyr de Hory, the Greatest Art Forger of Our Time* by Clifford Irving; *The Art Forger's Handbook* by Eric Hebborn; and *The Bright Shapes and the True Names: A Memoir* by Patrick McCaughey.

I'd like to thank the Australia Council, Anna Robinson, Marie Trinchant (and her boyfriend, Enrique del Rey Cabero), Dr. Emily Jones, Gregory Mackay, Astred Hicks, Sonja Heijn, Nan McNab and Hilary Reynolds, as well as the marketing and sales team at Allen & Unwin for their help, support and enthusiasm.

Huge thanks to Elise Jones and Anna McFarlane for unparalleled editorial and publishing support — you took this book to a whole other level.

And finally, thanks to Dominique, Harry, Charlie and Andrew. The guy, the girl, the artist, his ex and I couldn't have done any of it without you.

GABRIELLE WILLIAMS has three kids, one husband and a dog. She is the author of the critically acclaimed *Beatle Meets Destiny* (shortlisted for the Prime Minister's Literary Awards and Victorian Premier's Literary Awards) and *The Reluctant Hallelujah* (short-listed for the Gold Inky Award). She has been described by *The Age* reviewer Cameron Woodhead as "one of the funniest young adult fiction authors around." As part of her research for *The Guy, the Girl, the Artist and His Ex*, Gab interviewed a number of people — some of who may or may not have been the actual Australian Cultural Terrorists.